LOOK WHAT THE E-MAILS DID

Maddie Conway

Glitterati

Amouras – The
messenger of love

Carrotpeaaash

Turnipear

The Bodyguards

4

LOOK WHAT THE E-MAILS DID

Maddie Conway

This edition published 2018 by Carrowmore

ISBN: 978-1-9999915-7-9

Carrowmore Publishing
www.carrowmore.ie
info@carrowmore.ie
@Carrowmore101

Design and Layout
Dennison Design
Rock Street, Kenmare, Co Kerry
www.dennisondesign.ie
hello@dennisondesign.ie

Liame — The e-mail boss

Jason - The earthling

Potatodai - banished sentry and loyal friend

Zamba - The Strawberry Princess

Jackeus Frostus

Liame, boss of the E-mail Corporation, was in a horrible mood and no amount of sweet-talking was going to get him out of it. He was completely and utterly exhausted after a hectic week's work – and now this!

'*Mr Liame, sir,*' whimpered the little e-mail messenger sitting at his feet. '*Mr Liame, I have something to tell you.*'

'*What is it Importento?*' asked Liame, in an impatient tone. '*Has there been a crash in the sky?*'

'*No, sir, nothing like that at all. It's the Paparasky, the space reporters who follow us e-mails all over the sky looking for news to sell to their sky space newspapers.*'

Liame sat bolt upright in his chair. '*Oh no!*' he moaned. '*Please do not tell me that one of you lot dropped an e-mail message. And, please do not tell me that the Paparasky have gotten hold of it. Your duty as e-mails is to serve the earthlings and the earthlings only. All the e-mail messages travelling from one computer to another are confidential. Your job is to take them out of the computer outbox and bring them to the other person's inbox. Do you understand me?*'

'*Yes, yes sir,*' the little e-mail replied in a timid voice. '*Your wish is our command, sir.*'

However, Liame had not finished. '*It is unfortunate that you e-mails have to bounce to the tip-top of the sky and bounce back down in order to get a message from one earthling computer to another. I wish it did not work like that. Maybe technology will get better in time and then we will not have to travel so far upwards.*'

'No, no, no!' wailed Importento. 'You have it all wrong, Mr Liame, sir. It is just that my friend Dee, the cherub with the lilac sparkly wings, told me that one of our e-mail staff was kidnapped by the Paparasky.'

'An e-mail? Kidnapped! Which e-mail?' roared Liame. 'Give me the name at once.'

'It's Amouras, the Love Mail,' whispered Importento. 'The cherub told me that Amouras was kidnapped by the Paparasky and brought to Planet Zibazilia, that strange planet way up at the tip-top of the sky. Dee thinks that the Zibazilians want him so they can find out information about the earthlings. They may be planning an invasion.'

A tiny dribble of sweat began to emerge on Liame's forehead. 'Typical,' he groaned. 'No doubt the Paparasky are looking for some reward from the Zibazilians if they brought him there. All sky-dwellers despise the Paparasky. I bet they set this up to make a story for their stupid sky space newspapers.'

Liame began to swing his antennae back and forth. A few minutes passed before he spoke again. 'Amouras the Love e-mail is one of the most important e-mail staff that I have. What would the earthlings do if they were unable to e-mail messages of love to one another? Importento, you may be the President's e-mail messenger, but for today and tomorrow, I want you to find out everything you can about the kidnapping, and report to me every hour. Do you hear me? This is a terrible tragedy. We must call a meeting at once and start to gather some more information.'

'Yes, Mr Liame, sir,' quivered Importento, suddenly remembering that he had a very urgent e-mail to deliver from the President to his head chef. The President had decided that he wanted strawberry ice cream instead of vanilla for his after-dinner treat. It would have to wait. After all, Liame had spoken and Liame was head of the entire e-mail corporation. When Liame wanted something, everybody jumped.

It was a chilly October night. Way, way up at the very top of the sky, Princess Zamba, Strawberry Princess and ruler of Planet Zibazilia stood on tippy toes at her red, sparkly, strawberry-shaped dressing table. She carefully placed her gold and diamanté tiara onto her head. This tiara was used only for very special occasions, and tonight was one of those very special occasions.

It had been an exciting day for the little Princess. Newskeea, head of the Paparasky had made an appointment to see her. He had in his company a very important guest.

It was a guest who knew all about Planet Earth and would, Newskeea claimed, be able to offer advice. In return, the Paparasky had requested an interview with Princess Zamba. This would be the first interview ever with an inhabitant of Planet Zibazilia.

'I've been kidnapped, Princess!' wailed Amouras, as he clung tightly to a large envelope. *'Please let me go, I have a message of love to deliver.'*

Princess Zamba could not take her eyes off the little e-mail who sat on the ground at her feet. He had a heart-shaped body and the big envelope was attached to his little tummy. 'Oh, my golly gosh' she gasped. *'You look so pretty. Of course, you must not think that you have been kidnapped. Don't be a silly billy.'*

'But I have, Princess!' wailed Amouras.

Princess Zamba smiled sweetly. *'The Paparasky said that you would be delighted to come to Planet Zibazilia and tell me all about Planet*

Earth. I would love to know how the earthlings live, what they do, and why they are so tall. They told me you were a sort of an e-mail postal worker. We do not have computers or e-mails up here, so I would be so chuffed if you would tell me about your job and about the earthlings.'

Amouras sniffled. He had never met a live princess before; why did he have to make a fool of himself and cry! After all, she was ever so pretty, and she smelled good too.

Princess Zamba played with a strand of her golden hair. *'I want to visit Planet Earth and I want to invite an earthling up to our planet. Do you understand little e-mail?'*

Amouras shifted uncomfortably on the rather itchy rug. *'I am only a messenger for the earthlings ma'am,'* he quivered. *'It is true that my buddies and I carry e-mail messages for them, but we are only tiny in comparison to them. Can't you see that we are only a few centimetres in height?'*

The Princess beckoned her visitor to come forward. *'How tall are these earthlings? I have heard so many different stories and I do not know which to believe.'*

Amouras moved forward as instructed. *'Princess, the earthlings are giants, some of them seven feet in height. I only hang around the earthling houses long enough to collect the e-mail messages from their computers and then I am off. If the earthlings delete us, then our careers are over and we just wander the sky. That is what happened to several of our spam carriers who didn't check the type of message they were carrying before they left the computer.'*

Princess Zamba was not listening. *'As you can see, the people of Planet Zibazilia are only nine inches tall,'* she explained. *'That is why I want to meet an earthling. I want to find out what they eat and why they are so tall. If we changed our diet here, we might get bigger and stronger. Then, if inhabitants of another planet invaded, we could protect ourselves.'*

'Did you know, Amouras, that five hundred and fifty-one years and two days ago there was a hurricane on Planet Earth?'

'No, ma'am – I mean Princess,' mumbled Amouras.

'Did you know that heaps of seeds from plants, fruits, and vegetables were blown all the way up here, and that is where we came from? The Zibazilians are descendants of the plants, vegetables, and fruits of Planet Earth? Isn't that something?'

'No, Princess, I had no idea that your people originally came from Planet Earth,' whispered Amouras in a hoarse voice, as he wiped a bead of sweat from his heart-shaped forehead. *'The earthlings must not know this, otherwise they would be sending e-mails like me up to you with messages.'*

Finally, Amouras began to relax, and he and the Princess ended up chatting for hours. Amouras told Princess Zamba what he knew about the earthlings, but he was unable to let her know in which direction Planet Earth lay. He explained to her that the tiny antennae on his head directed him there; they sent him to the top of the sky with an e-mail message but when he bounced back down, the antennae told him where to go.

At last he said to the Princess, *'I wish I could tell you more. Now please, can you tell the Paparasky to release me and allow me to go back to my home? My boss and the other e-mails will be so worried about me. And also, I'm cooking dinner tonight.'*

Even from the little information she got, Princess Zamba promised the Paparasky an interview, on the condition that they would drop Amouras off where they had found him in the sky. *'Such a sweet little creature,'* she sighed. She had loved every moment of his visit and she was now even more determined to visit Planet Earth. It was all so terribly exciting!

After the interview and the departure of her special guest, Princess Zamba found herself in a massive state of excitement. Her tummy kept doing somersaults and she simply could not rest. She decided to visit her friend Potatodai, who was on sentry duty on the north edge of Zibazilia.

Way, way down through the palace gardens, the little Princess scurried, on one winding path and then another. It began to rain quite heavily, so she stood against a large rock for shelter. The rainwater squelched in and out of her golden strawberry slippers, but she did not care. She tucked her long golden hair underneath the hood of her strawberry cape. Thankfully, the rain began to ease off after a few minutes, so she continued on her mission.

'Potatodai!' she beamed excitedly as she made her way closer to him. 'Potatodai, my dear friend, I am so excited to see you.'

Potatodai wiped a raindrop from the Princess's beautiful strawberry eyes. 'Something must be terribly wrong, Your Sweet Highness, for you to come out here on such a bad night,' he said. 'Are you feeling unwell?'

The little Princess smiled as caring Potatodai found shelter for her under a rock with a protruding top.

'Dear, dear Potatodai, my loyal sentry and friend,' she whispered.

'Before we begin our conversation, I would like to tell you that it makes me so very sad to have to watch you out here on sentry duty every night of the week and in all types of weather. I am Zamba, Strawberry Princess of Zibazilia, and your friend. It upsets me to *think that I, as a Princess, am unable to help you. It is cold, and it is miserable for a good part of the year, and my heart bleeds so badly for you. I wish somebody could take your place and give you some nights off. It is all so unfair.'*

Potatodai smiled gratefully. *'Your Royal Highness and my good friend Princess Zamba, I thank you for your great concern, but I must accept my punishment and hope that good things are to come. We both know that many years ago, I gave wrong directions to a passing star and that everybody was worried that she would fall into enemy hands in the sky.*

'Of course, I also know that your two bodyguards, Turnipear and Carrotpeaash, were jealous of me and decided at the time that I should no longer be a bodyguard, but that I should be a sentry instead.'

Princess Zamba sniffled a little and wiped a tear from her eye. *'I have tried so hard to sort this out,'* she sobbed quietly. *'But Turnipear and Carrotpeaash are descendants of one of our past rulers, and it is said that they have had unusual powers handed down to them.*

'I would be scared to go against their wishes. If I reinstate you as a bodyguard, I fear the worst. Then again, it might just be a rumour, maybe they have no extraordinary powers. How am I to know whether it is the truth or not? I must also consider the fact they are both so good to me, I would hate to have a row with them. They cater for my every need and make sure I am short of nothing. I find myself in such an awkward situation. Some day, dear Potatodai, I will find a way to have you back in favour again, just you wait and see.'

Potatodai blushed. It was seldom Princess Zamba, the ruler of Zibazilia, poured her strawberry heart out to him. Now he had to find out what the little Princess had really come to talk about. She would certainly not have crept out behind her bodyguard's back unless she really needed to pick his brains.

'I had a visitor today, Potatodai,' she whispered sweetly. 'His name was Amouras the e-mail. He delivers computer e-mail messages for the earthlings. This messenger carries messages of love. The Papurusky brought him to me. We made a deal. In return for them bringing him to me, I promised to give them an interview to sell to the Universal Space Newspaper.'

Potatodai was intrigued. 'Go on, Your Highness, tell me more.'

'Based on the information the little e-mail messenger gave me, I've made my people a promise, but I don't know if I was wise in doing that. I told them that I would organise a trip to Planet Earth. We hear about Planet Earth when Kaoisa the space pumpkin comes to tea.'

'Yes, Princess, that is true,' answered Potatodai politely.

The Princess continued in a very low whisper. 'Kaoisa bounces his way down there on Halloween night every year. However, you know he has a musty brain and cannot memorise many details. Now this dear little e-mail has given me more information. But, having thought further about it, I now know that I should have consulted you before I made this promise to my people.'

Potatodai was puzzled. 'Why have you not consulted Carrotpeaash and Turnipear about this matter, dear Princess? They are your bodyguards and far more important than I am.'

Princess Zamba sighed and did not answer.

'Think about it!' he continued. 'They are your bodyguards, and I – I am nobody, just a banished sentry and night watchman.'

Princess Zamba shifted from one foot to the other in an uncomfortable fashion. 'I did mention it to them earlier, but they laughed in my face,' she confessed. 'They said I should not dream of the impossible. Planet Earth keeps moving around and around, so they tell me it would be impossible for us to find it.

'However, I am Princess and leader of Planet Zibazilia and I feel it is my duty to meet our ancestors, the earthlings. Amouras the e-mail told me that the earthlings are very clever and that they have very pretty faces and very pretty clothes. He said that they eat large amounts of food and that is why they are so tall. Maybe on their advice we should change our diet. It worries me that they eat veggies and fruit that look like us. He did suggest eating food called meat or fish.'

'Maybe your bodyguards are right, Your Royal Highness,' Potatodai ventured. *'Maybe you are looking at the impossible! They are only trying to protect you. Moreover, dear Princess, if they find out that you came to me for assistance they will be more than annoyed. You know they have banished me.'*

Princess Zamba had not been listening to a single word. *'I will be the envy of all the other planets if I bring an earthling to visit,'* she giggled. *'Oh, gilly golly gosh. It is all so very exciting. Can't you just see it on all the sky space newspaper headlines? "Planet Zibazilia Welcomes Earthling!"*

'Do not escort me back, dear Potatodai. I would like some time on my own before I enter the castle.'

'Your Highness, the earthlings are six foot tall, and we are all less than nine inches. They could eat us up, could swallow us in one bite!' roared Potatodai. *'We look like mixed-up fruit and vegetables, and they eat those.'*

His words had fallen on deaf ears. *'And, Planet Earth is zillions of miles away and we are not sure even in which direction it lies. Are you aware that months of preparation would need to go in this journey?'* he shouted into the night sky.

But as he watched her scurry away at speed, Potatodai was happy to see the adorable little Princess in such a happy mood. At that very moment he made up his mind that he would do anything at all he could do to help. He was willing to resort to drastic measures if he had to, but he hoped it would not come to that.

He loved Princess Zamba and wanted to please her. Secretly, the thought of meeting the earthlings also excited him.
However, he had to keep his head planted firmly on his shoulders and not get carried away with the idea. Of course, if he did manage to help the Princess, maybe she would find a way of having him reinstated as a bodyguard. He had a lot of deep thinking to do before he met her again.

Potatodai didn't sleep after he went to bed that morning, in fact he did not sleep for three whole days. He just tossed and turned, and then turned and tossed. He had a pain in his chest with worry and his head oozed with questions. Was it far too risky to take a Ziggercraft on an unknown voyage? Would it make the long journey? How much zonk could it hold? Would the humans think the crew were some kind of exotic fruit and gobble them up? After all, the Zibazilians did look like a mixture of fruits, plants, and vegetables, and they smelled ever so good. Princess Zamba herself looked and smelled like a strawberry, and who could possibly resist a pretty strawberry? All these questions remained unanswered.

In addition to all of these fears, there was another serious worry. Planet Zibazilia only had one powerful Ziggercraft. If this craft got stranded on Earth there would be no way to send down a rescue team. The two smaller Ziggercrafts were only pleasure crafts used for visiting neighbouring friendly planets. They could only travel for thirty space miles before having to refuel and have the craft's small engine oiled.

Problems, problems and more problems zigzagged through Potatodai's brain. As soon as he thought he had solved one, another appeared. Since his conversation with Princess Zamba, there had only been one or two sightings of her. This concerned him deeply. Her little face wore a tired and strained look, and it was obvious her bodyguards had instructed her to stay indoors. Potatodai hoped that she would get sensible advice from Turnipear and Carrotpeaash. It was obvious that they had found out about her visit and had strongly advised her not to consult with anybody but them.

The next night Potatodai had a brainwave, the most fabulous mega-brainwave ever. Why had it not occurred to him before? He thought it would never be daylight. He needed to consult his friend Glitterati, leader of the stars. Glitterati would surely be able to help, but he travelled the skies by night with his team of stars, and so Potatodai would have to wait for him until daybreak.

Finally, after what seemed like an age, he spied the first group of stars making their weary way home. Glitterati would be last. Potatodai knew this, because his friend would never leave the sky until he had collected every single one of his workers. He was terrified one of them could get left behind and he knew that stars could not function during daylight hours. Daylight made their eyes weep and they became extremely disorientated.

At last, Glitterati arrived, glowing with brightness and happiness from point to point. *'Hello Potatodai, old buddy, you okay?'* he yelled. *'And how are all my friends on Planet Zibazilia?'*

Glitterati and Potatodai had been friends for many years. Glitterati hated to see his pal out in the bad weather doing sentry duty. Often, they tried to think up a way that would make Turnipear and Carrotpeaash change their mind, but they could never come up with anything good enough. Only for his friend Glitterati, Potatodai knew that he would never survive the long cold nights of winter. It was good to have such a nice friend, very good indeed.

'Potatodai, I'm excited because you're excited,' giggled Glitterati. *'It is seldom I find you in this state. Go on,'* he begged. *'Tell me what this is all about.'* After carefully bending his corners underneath him, Glitterati sat himself down and listened intently to his friend's story.

The tale impressed him greatly. *'It would be wonderful, Potatodai, if I could help to find a solution to the Princess's problem,'* he said. *'Leave it with me for a few days. I will search my starry brain for bright and gleaming ideas.'*

'Yes, yes it would,' agreed Potatodai. 'It might even make Turnipear and Carrotpeaash see me in a different light. They may even find it in their hearts to forgive me. I do not care if they take all the credit for it. All I want is to have my life back.'

Glitterati wiped a piece of dew from his forehead. 'Don't be daft Potatodai; those two are jealous of you. You had better believe it. You were born with brains and they were not. All they can boast about is that they had some relatives with powers. Your Princess told me that you have more brains than the two of them put together. Leave the matter with me for a couple of hours and I will be back to you.'

On that note, Glitterati departed. It had been a busy night, so he rolled up his corners and fell asleep the minute he arrived back at his cave.

It was his fourth day of no sleep, so Potatodai made himself a glass of vivu, a herbal drink that helped him get a few hours' sleep. This evening, he would go to work early and meet Glitterati before he and his stars departed into the skies for the night. He hoped Glitterati would have thought of something.

'You didn't come up with a solution, did you?' Potatodai moaned in a gloomy voice as Glitterati approached that evening.

'And how did I get to be in charge of all these stars if I am not a good planner?' Glitterati joked. 'I had a long think and guess what: I did come up with something.'

Potatodai did a double somersault with excitement. 'I knew it!' he cheered. 'I knew I could rely on you.'

'Not too fast, my friend, it is only an idea,' giggled Glitterati.

'I love your ideas,' squealed Potatodai with delight. 'You always have good ones.'

Glitterati grinned again. *'Thank you, Potatodai, and now let me tell you this new idea. I searched my starry brain and I remembered a conversation I had with one of my junior stars on her way home one night about a year ago. Aza is the star's name. She had gone missing for a few days and I was going to give her a telling off, but she was in a terrible state of shock when I finally found her, she was barely able to speak.*

'Aza explained that she had gotten tangled in another star as they had stayed too close together, chatting in the sky. When she finally untangled herself, she lost her balance, fell downwards, and was unable to turn herself around. She claimed she was falling for quite a number of days. But, while Aza was falling, she noticed something very, very strange.'

'Go on, go on tell me what she saw,' begged Potatodai, who was almost too excited to speak. *'What did Aza see?'*

Glitterati smiled once more. He had never seen Potatodai so wound up about anything and he was so thrilled that he was the bearer of some good news.

'Okay,' he said. *'Aza remembered falling towards a big round planet full of water and mountains, and big, big giants. I consulted Old Man Time and, lo and behold, her description matched Planet Earth. She was so glad that she had stopped herself from falling before she fell down into this strange land.'*

Potatodai was puzzled. *'How did she stop herself falling? Did someone help her?'*

Glitterati beamed. *'You would never believe it but she was saved by a beautiful cherub. It was a cherub called Kika. Aza described her has having big sparkly wings and the chubbiest cheeks she had ever seen. She smelt of roses. Kika came out of nowhere, lifted Aza with her wing, and allowed her to float upwards again. The cherub told her that stars never went to Earth. It was their duty to give light to Earth and allow the earthlings to see when it got dark. Only for that cherub, my star could easily have gotten kidnapped.'*

'Or she could have burned up!' Potatodai chimed in. *'She had a very, very lucky escape. Do you think I could have a word with her? I need to know the exact direction in which Planet Earth lies.'*

Glitterati shook his head. *'It is not possible to meet her. Aza got such a fright when this happened. She lost her confidence to go into the sky again. I gave her special pardon. She now does some administration work for me, and a fine job she is making of it, too. However, I did ask her in what direction Planet Earth lies and she has given me very clear directions.'*

Potatodai was confused. *'But … but how could she remember the directions? Planet Earth is so far away. I think she may be telling you a little fib, Glitterati.'*

Glitterati very quickly defended his star. *'Now, now, don't jump to conclusions, Potatodai. Let me explain. That beautiful cherub invited Aza to come to tea some evening and so she gave her a very special map of the sky before she left. Aza has shown this precious document to very few people. However, I told her your story and she has given a loan of the map to me.*

'But I must go now, Potatodai. I have a busy night ahead.'

It was well after eight in the morning when Potatodai finally fell into a deep, happy sleep. He was so excited he even forgot to put on his little lavender bed socks. Since chatting with Princess Zamba days previously, he was having frequent dreams about giants and goblins, and all kinds of weird things.

In one of these dreams, he found himself in the fist of a giant, about to be squashed and eaten, when a cherub came along and gave the giant one big beam of a smile. The giant was so excited that he forgot what he was doing for a brief second and Potatodai escaped.

'Psst … psst … are you there, Potatodai, sir? The Princess wants a meeting with you,' whispered a little voice.

Potatodai blinked, quite unsure as to whether he was awake or asleep or in the middle of another strange dream.

'Psst … psst,' came the voice again. 'Answer me, please. I must not be seen down here.'

The colourful uniform of the page standing beside Potatodai's hammock quickly knocked the sleep out of his eyes.

'What is it, Zazak?' Potatodai asked.

'It's the Princess,' said the little onionfern in a louder whisper. *'She wants to know if you have any news for her.'*

'Oh, yes,' answered Potatodai happily. *'I have great news for her. Your timing is just right. Shall I go to her now?'*

'No, no, no!' shrieked the little page. *'Neither you nor any of the servants who live down here are allowed to the top quarters of our palace without special permission. You should know that. Turnipear and Carrotpeaash have set the rules. It is for safety reasons. Only the four other pages Zipa, Zope, Zind, Zoho and I are allowed to move about the palace, and even then, only if we are on official duty.'*

'Then tell her to come to me tonight when the clock strikes twelve,' whispered Potatodai. *'Tell her I will stand on the very tallest rock over at the north side of our planet. Tell her to wrap up warmly, as the nights are very cold. Tell her if she can't sneak out tonight that I will wait at that rock at midnight for her each night this week.'*

The little page scurried away with his news. Potatodai did not sleep a wink after that. He just swung in his hammock and daydreamed of visiting Planet Earth. He dreamt of getting the giants who lived down there to come up and persuade Turnipear and Carrotpeaash to let him be part of the palace again.

In his daydream, the earthling giants put their big feet on top of the heads of the bodyguards and threatened to squash them in to the ground unless they allowed him to have his royal duties back again. Then one giant threw a spit at Carrotpeaash and it knocked him to the ground. It was all so funny.

Evening came quickly and Potatodai waited patently for midnight to arrive. Five minutes past midnight came, then twenty minutes, and then thirty minutes. The little Princess had not arrived.

Potatodai decided not to fret. He suspected that his beloved Princess was waiting until the coast was clear and her bodyguards were asleep. Finally, the scent of strawberry wafted through the air and Potatodai quickly beckoned the Princess behind a very large rock.

'Over here, your Royal Sweet Highness,' he called out in his loudest whisper. 'I have brought a snowdrop rug to wrap around you.'

Princess Zamba could not contain her excitement as Potatodai told her the story of Aza star.

'I can even tell you the direction of Planet Earth,' he beamed. 'It may not be impossible to get there after all. Of course, there are so many more problems to be ironed out before we could think of trying…'

'You have such brains, Potatodai. You have more brains than the rest of us put together,' beamed Princess Zamba.

'No, Your Highness,' Potatodai reminded her. 'I was just given information from a star that got lost and almost landed on Earth. I'm not that brainy.'

Once again, the little Princess was far too excited to listen. 'I must thank the Paparasky for bringing that e-mail here,' she beamed. 'That sweet little creature made me realise what a wonderful place Planet Earth is.'

Princess Zamba continued to jump up and down, and her golden slippers glistened in the moonlight. 'Giants five or six feet tall!' she screamed. 'I know Old Man Time told me this, but I thought he was exaggerating. Oh my gilly golly gosh! I want to meet these people and find out all their secrets. I want my people to be big, strong and tall, just like they are.

'I need to find out what they eat, where they sleep, and all sorts of other things. Our people have no weapons, so we need to be big and strong to protect ourselves and our planet. All the planets around us have guns. They could invade us at any time if they felt like it. Even you, Potatodai, could not prevent an attack. Also, I want to meet the people of Earth because we originally came from there.'

'Please, sweet Princess,' begged Potatodai. *'Please take more time to think this whole matter out. Those giants on Earth must be feared until we find out more about them. If they eat their own fruit, who is to say that they won't gobble us down too?'*

'We are different. They surely will not touch us. Oh, my gilly golly gosh, if we find out what those giants eat, we could be tall too. Maybe we are eating the wrong food! Oh my golly gissy giss,' she squealed again, as she danced up and down. *'I must go and give Turnipear and Carrotpeaash the good news.'*

Potatodai rubbed his head with amazement. *'But … but Your Sweet Highness, they will be very angry when they find out you have confided in me once again. I thought the whole idea was that you would not let them know that you had consulted me.*

'You should find a more discreet way of telling them. Could I suggest that you use the name of Kaoisa the space pumpkin? Tell them he told you.'

Yet again the Princess was far too excited to hear anything. She blew Potatodai a tiny strawberry-shaped kiss and then disappeared in to the night.

'Yinny lanno wooo,' she sang, as she skipped back to the palace. She was even too excited to notice two young Zibazilians snogging in a corner of the palace, which was strictly out of bounds. The smaller one, a lemon honeysuckle, tucked her little face underneath her boyfriend's coat and giggled. They were in love and not even their Princess was going to change that.

'I love you,' she whispered, *'I love you, I love you, I love you, and I don't care if the Princess saw us.'*

Her boyfriend, a skinny sweetpea dandelion, chuckled and snuggled up closer to her. *'I don't care either,'* he replied. *'I love you too, I love you too.'*

'*Carrotpeaash, Turnipear, where are you?*' Princess Zamba yelled. '*We will have a meeting in my chambers now. I hope you are not asleep!*'

Turnipear was sitting on the corridor. He wore a large, ugly scowl on his face.

'*Your royal highness,*' he spluttered, suddenly standing to attention. '*I did not know that you had snuck out of your chambers. I am a little concerned that you did not inform me. You must understand it is my job – and of course Carrotpeaash's, too – to protect you. I worry that untrustworthy Potatodai has put bad ideas into you head.*'

Princess Zamba threw one of her tiny wet squishy slippers and her cape onto a chair. '*Turnipear, Turnipear, Turnipear, you worry too much,*' she beamed. '*Please forgive me. I took a crazy notion to visit Potatodai. I know you think he is not to be trusted but he has great knowledge of the skies and with the help of some of his friends he has come back with some useful information.*'

'*And what sort of information is that?*' Turnipear scowled in a sarcastic tone.

'*It looks as if we will be able to visit Planet Earth after all!*' whooped Princess Zamba.

Turnipear bowed and hung the Princess's wet cape on the coat stand. '*Whatever makes Your Royal Highness happy,*' he murmured in a low voice. '*Whatever makes you happy makes me happy, too. We will discuss this matter further in the morning.*

'Nevertheless, you must realise that we are here to protect you. Our duty is to see that no harm comes to you. You cannot afford to take chances.'

It had been an exciting night. Potatodai was pleased but a little worried. He was pleased that he had made the Princess happy, but he was concerned that his ideas would go down like a lead balloon with the bodyguards. If only they would come to him to talk about it. After all, they would get all the glory for organising the trip. All Potatodai wanted was to regain their trust and become part of his people again.

The rain continued to pour down for hours but Potatodai did not even notice; nothing was going to spoil this very exciting night.

Each of the Ziggercraft's engines revved in turn, as a dandelionasparagus mechanic did the final tests. The Ziggercraft was multicoloured and shaped like a wrinkly dog. Each wrinkle folded into a seat. The seats were so comfy that some passengers fell asleep seconds after take off. Only a few hours now, and this Ziggercraft would make the longest and most exciting journey ever made in the history of Planet Zibazilia. This Ziggercraft was about to travel all the way to Planet Earth.

In the distance, Potatodai watched all the excitement with a heavy heart. A full week had gone by and his Princess had not come to visit him again. He wondered why, and he began to fret very badly. What if they did not consult him or bring him with them? He was the only one except Aspalemon the pilot who had any knowledge of the skies.

Aspalemon was highly excitable and would not, Potatodai feared, be able to cope under extreme pressure on his own. In addition to this, Aspalemon had only flown a few miles from one adjoining planet to another before, so he too lacked experience.

Potatodai wished that he could advise Princess Zamba to postpone the journey to Planet Earth until he had done some more research into it. They needed to consider how much fuel and food to take, and many other matters. His stomach did somersaults, and he could not rest anywhere. It was such a horrible situation and he found himself powerless.

The hours dragged by so slowly as Potatodai waited for the moment of take off. Pangs of guilt shot up and down in his stomach. Maybe he should not have encouraged the little Princess.

Maybe he should not have given her the information she wanted. Was he sending her to her death? The very thought almost made him sick. He wished with all his heart that the whole thing was nothing but a very long nightmare with a happy conclusion.

'Zope! Zope!' he called to the smallest page, who was picking some space-berries and was only too delighted to talk.

'It's tonight at midnight,' the little page informed him. *'That is when the Ziggercraft will take off. It is all so exciting, isn't it? Princess Zamba asked me to make up some rooms in case we have visitors from Earth soon. I did suggest that giants would not fit in our palace, but nobody wanted to listen. I suppose we could build something for them outside! Remember, we are nine inches and they are giants,'* he squeaked.

'I suppose we could,' agreed Potatodai, as he glanced sadly across the sky.

As nightfall approached, Potatodai went about his nightly duties. He decided to watch the take off from a safe distance, from one of the tallest rocks.

'What's going on?' he asked the little page who ran towards him, waving a sheet of paper.

'It's the Princess!' shrieked the page. *'She wants to speak to you this minute. Hurry, please.'*

'Are you sure?' asked Potatodai. *'It's unusual for servants or sentries to get an invite up to the chambers of Her Royal Highness.'*

The little page bowed. *'The Princess has spoken, and we must obey. Please, follow me.'*

Princess Zamba sat on her diamanté armchair, looking radiant. The tips of the outside lashes of her eyes curled upwards, as if they were watching something. Tiny coloured, sparkly decorations adorned her hair. Her splendid tiara sat on a red cushion at her feet. She wore the most wonderful red cloak, made from the shells of space beetles and held together with delicate golden threads. It made a strange sound as she moved. Sentries and pages stood everywhere. Little plates of delicacies sat on small tables here and there throughout the room. An air of calm and mystery filled the whole area.

'Sit down, Potatodai, sit down,' Princess Zamba chirped happily. 'Today is such a wonderful day.'

'It is, Your Royal Highness,' echoed both Turnipear and Carrotpeaash, as they bowed together. They seemed genuinely pleased to see Potatodai.

'Yes, please sit down,' echoed Turnipear, doing his best to smile. Carrotpeaash never smiled. That was understandable, as it would take a while to thaw out his stern face. By the time it thawed out, the happy or funny moment would have passed.

Potatodai's heart missed a beat. Maybe, just maybe, the bodyguards were going to reconsider. Maybe this visit to Earth was the best thing that ever happened.

Princess Zamba smiled. 'Potatodai, my good and loyal sentry, I have something to tell you.'

'I'm all ears, Your Highness,' Potatodai mumbled nervously.

Princess Zamba placed a tiny piece of bat nougat on to the front of her tongue. It had quite a delicious smell. She licked her strawberry lips twice and then she spoke. *'Turnipear, Carrotpeaash, and I have decided that your good self, Aspalemon the pilot, and twelve helpers will go on this exciting journey to Planet Earth. On this occasion, I myself will not go. Instead, we will use this visit as a fact-finding mission for bigger things to come.'*

Potatodai's two legs began to wobble. He directed his gaze at the two bodyguards, who both wore big smiles. This was all too much to take in. Carrotpeaash was actually trying to force a smile and the little Princess was not going to Planet Earth. Two weird things were happening at once. Had everybody suddenly gone crazy?

'But ... but Turnipear and Carrotpeaash you – you're not going, I don't understand! I thought you would not miss this moment for anything!' Potatodai blubbered.

Turnipear answered without hesitation: *'We have decided to stay here and look after our Princess. It is up to you to go to Planet Earth first and let us know whether it is safe or not. On your return, we may then consider taking our Royal Highness with us. We have had a long chat about this, and Carrotpeaash and I agreed we would never forgive ourselves if something happened to the Princess while we were down on Planet Earth.'*

Carrotpeaash continued in a small voice: *'You are an expert of the skies because of all the time you spend on sentry duty. You are, on this occasion, more qualified than we are to make the journey. However, we expect that you will not leave a stone unturned, and that you will come back with every detail on the earthlings. We want to know what they eat, what they do all day, where they get their brains, and many other things, of course. Do not come back until you know everything.'*

Princess Zamba smiled proudly at Potatodai and then flicked her little finger at Turnipear, her senior bodyguard and adviser.

'You did mention earlier that if Potatodai has a successful mission you will consider relieving him of most of his sentry duty…'

Turnipear shuffled uncomfortably, then spoke in a loud, assertive voice: 'That is correct, Your Highness. That is exactly what we agreed. We will certainly cut down on his duties if his mission is a success. We will then find another sentry who, by doing a few nights a week, will allow Potatodai much more time off.'

Potatodai was quietly overjoyed. 'Thank you, everybody,' he mumbled, quite unsure what else to say. 'That means so much to me. I will do all I can to make the voyage a success. However, Turnipear and Carrotpeaash, I will gladly accept any advice you can give me. I would be honoured to have even one of you on this journey with me.'

Turnipear cleared his throat and spoke, while pacing up and down the room: 'Thank you for the kind thought. However, it would be very unwise for everybody senior to leave Planet Zibazilia, and to leave the Princess without a bodyguard. In fact, one of us alone would not be enough to guard our Princess. We do hope you understand.'

Potatodai was puzzled; it was not often the two bodyguards would turn down a big opportunity like this. If the mission was a success, they would both receive the highest honours. It was all rather confusing. Or was it?

'Beneath their thick skins, they are two cowards and are probably too scared to make the journey. They do not care if I run in to danger. I'll show them I can do it,' Potatodai thought to himself. 'They think I am a fool, but I am a lot smarter and stronger than they are.'

Princess Zamba glowed with an air of strawberry, princessy happiness. 'This is all so positive. I'm in a happy, happy mood,' she chirped. 'I'll talk to you all later. Turnipear and Carrotpeaash, please have a long chitty-chat with Potatodai and make sure he has everything he wants. And when I say everything, I mean everything.'

Both bodyguards bowed and nodded. *'Certainly, Your Royal Highness,'* they echoed. *'We will give him as much help as he needs. We will take him to the big reception room and we will have a long discussion about everything. Your wish, Your Royal Highness, is our command.'*

The ice blue reception room was cool and inviting, and Potatodai began to relax. Carrotpeaash brought him a sweet drink and Turnipear tried hard to be nice.

'How much food and zonk have you loaded on to the Ziggercraft?' asked Potatodai.

'It won't be enough,' he said, on hearing their answer, but both convinced him that they had done a lot of research into the journey, and that the craft would topple over if they brought anymore zonk or food.

'This journey is very important for our Princess; do you think that we would leave you short food and zonk, and ruin this important visit?' they insisted. *'We are on your side, Potatodai. We may have banished you to do sentry duty, but it was for the good of our Princess. You gave wrong advice to a star and we felt you were not suitable to advise or guard Her Royal Highness anymore. Please forgive us but we do still love you.'*

For the second time that afternoon Potatodai began to relax. Maybe, just maybe, the bodyguards made sense. Maybe they were not so horrible after all and maybe it should be a lesson to him not to judge people before he spent time getting to know them well.

The discussion continued, and Potatodai tried his best to convince the bodyguards that the journey would take at least six to ten days, but they disagreed, and said that the craft would complete its journey in less than two.

'Your imagination is running away with you,' they argued. *'Our Ziggercraft is fast – it's one of the most powerful in all the planets around the area. Do not be such a pessimist.'*

'But how do you know?' asked Potatodai. *'You have not been in contact with anyone who has been to Earth by craft and the Ziggercraft has not undergone a long journey like this one.'*

Both bodyguards shook their heads. Carrotpeaash began to scratch the ash sprig that hung from his left ear. *'We have been wise in our judgements before this. Please trust us,'* they said in unison. *'You always claim to want a bigger challenge than being a sentry. Now you are getting it, and you are still complaining.*

'This conversation is getting tiring, so run along, Potatodai. We are very busy. You have your instructions. At midnight, your mission begins. Be prepared and good luck. We are all behind you.'

'And one other thing!' roared Carrotpeaash. *'We are sending twelve crew members to give you every assistance, so please do not feel that we have neglected you.'*

'Why does he have to be so argumentative?' moaned Carrotpeaash in a very loud voice, as he and Turnipear made their way back to Princess Zamba's chambers.

'We have given him a big opportunity and he does not appreciate it a single bit,' agreed Turnipear. *'Just what is the universe coming to at all?'*

At exactly two minutes to midnight, Potatodai boarded the Ziggercraft. The younger crew members shrieked with excitement as they sank in to the blue soft spongy seats. It was the first journey most of them had taken on the large Ziggercraft. Some had never before left their home planet, Zibazilia.

'Wheezy deezy,' they whooped. *'We are going on an adventure. Lots of nice food and we are going to meet some earthling aliens. Maybe we will get some pressies.'*

Potatodai had a very, very bad feeling in the pit of his stomach and felt unable to embrace their excitement. If Turnipear and Carrotpeaash had missed an opportunity like this, it had to mean that they sensed great danger. Apart from Aspalemon, the rest of the crew were young, inexperienced and not of much use should problems occur. Turnipear and Carrotpeaash were taking no chances. If things went wrong, the crew would not prove a great loss.

A different inner voice told Potatodai that his imagination was running away with him. The bodyguards had fallen over backwards to help him. Why did he have to be so negative about everything? He wondered where all his confidence had gone. He now had one chance to prove himself and that was exactly what he was determined to do. It was time to forget all his worries and go full steam ahead to Planet Earth.

Princess Zamba stood on tippy toes at the triangular window of her luxurious strawberry-shaped bedroom. She waved a brightly coloured lizard-skin scarf out though a tiny pane of glass in the top left-hand corner.

'*It may be the last time I will ever see my Princess,*' thought Potatodai sadly. '*What if something goes wrong? A rescue will be impossible, as we do not have another powerful Ziggercraft.*' Whatever happened, he would always hold the memory of dear Princess Zamba standing at the window waving him off. She would be his tower of strength by day and through the cold nights on his long journey.

Turnipear and Carrotpeaash stood at the door of the Ziggercraft. Each, in turn, wished Potatodai well and thanked him for his bravery. He was a credit to Planet Zibazilia, they informed him. Carrotpeaash pushed a purple stone in to his hand. '*It's a Zuba stone,*' he growled, in a kindly sort of fashion. '*It brings luck to anyone who has it their possession. If you carry this, you will come back safely.*'

Turnipear then spoke: '*As you are aware: this is the first time anyone from Planet Zibazilia has travelled downwards in a spacecraft. You are making our history. Congratulations!*'

Potatodai blushed, unused to such praise.

'*And,*' continued Turnipear, '*this is the first time our Ziggercraft has gone on a long journey, and you, with the help of Aspalemon, are in charge.*'

Potatodai blushed again. If the bodyguards continued, he would end up with a swelled head, but he did know that what they said made sense. The large Ziggercraft had only travelled across the sky to nearby friendly planets. It was built in case Zibazilia was invaded and everyone would have to run for their lives.

Nobody thought in their wildest dreams that it would make its first long journey to, of all places, Planet Earth. Somewhere deep down in the pit of his stomach Potatodai was rather proud. Maybe his luck was about to take a turn for the best after all. '*Buckle up, everybody,*' he roared. '*Our adventure begins now. It is now full steam ahead to Planet Earth.*'

Vroom, vroom, vroom – a single white heavy puff of smoke, and then they were off. The engines revved, and the craft raced alongside the edge of Planet Zibazilia. It was a huge test of skill for Aspalemon to manoeuvre the craft between the sharp jagged rocks of Planet Zibazilia. One final blast from the engines, a last-minute wave, and they were gone. A trail of smoke and fumes drifted through the sky as the craft gradually disappeared downwards.

A few senior Zibazilians sat on a tall rock, waved them off with a few space kisses, and wished them well. It was comforting for Potatodai that he had a few friends left on the planet.

On Princess Zamba's instruction, an old beantomato scribe recorded details of this historical day. She was aware that Old Man Time would also make a record, but she wanted to be doubly certain that no detail of this exciting adventure would go unnoticed. Now all she could do was hope and hope and hope that everything would go according to plan.

Technology in the Ziggercraft was not advanced enough to allow contact with Planet Zibazilia, so Potatodai and his crew were all alone out in the big vast sky. The younger Zibazilians began to complain of boredom after staring out the window for a few hours. 'Will we soon be on Planet Earth?' they asked continually.

'I think it will take us a little longer,' Potatodai reassured them, as he tried to think up something to do which would keep them amused. Maybe tonight they would all play *'cherubs and elves'.* It was a board game where the two teams were stuck in a maze and the one who got out first won the game. (Neither the cherubs nor the elves were allowed to fly. They all had to walk from one place to another.)

As her maids prepared her for bed that night, a niggling thought crossed Princess Zamba's mind. She wondered if perhaps she had been wise in listening to her bodyguards. The right side of her nose twitched, and that always meant that she was worried about something. In fact, it got so twitchy that she had to keep rubbing it on the pillow, and she could not lie on her back for ages. The more she thought about it, the more she realised that Potatodai was right; very little preparation had gone in to the whole journey.

If her bodyguards had refused to go, then they, too, must have sensed danger.

Suddenly she began to tremble. What had she done? Had she gone mad? Had she sent her best friend in the whole world to his death? Now she understood why Turnipear and Carrotpeaash had refused to make this historic journey. They must have suspected that the whole thing would not work out. That's why they put so little preparation into it.

Along with Potatodai and Aspalemon, they had sent twelve of the least brainy Zibazilians, who could not help or use their brains in any way. All they wanted to do was have fun. When she thought about it a little longer, the Princess realised that these were twelve juniors that her bodyguards never had a good word to say about.

But, more importantly, what was this their plan to get rid of Potatodai, the brainiest Zibazilian and her dear, dear friend? Princess Zamba trembled with fear as she tried to have forty winks. And she also knew that she must keep her fears to herself. After all, Turnipear and Carrotpeaash were cousins of the great NettleElder. She heard that he had magical powers and could throw out a dangerous sting if he got mad. If his descendants were not treated with dignity, it was rumoured that the great NettleElder could send a curse from the grave.

Apart from this, the little Princess was aware that both Turnipear and Carrotpeaash loved her to bits and they treated her with the greatest of respect and made sure that everyone else did likewise. She, too, loved them both to bits, but she hated them for the way in which they treated Potatodai.

She also knew that she would not be safe without her bodyguards. They catered for her every need. It was all such a difficult situation. She wished there was no such a thing as jealousy. Jealousy was a terrible thing, and it made people do awful things. Maybe the earthlings might have some sort of medicine to get rid of jealousy. Yes, the matter was definitely worth looking in to.

Princess Zamba dismissed the colourful page who sat on the edge of her bed, ready to tell her a bedtime story. She was not in the mood. *'Have an early night,'* she whispered kindly to him. *'I am not in the mood for bedtime stories. I have many worries on my mind. Come back tomorrow night and you can tell me two different stories.'*

'Tomorrow is another day,' she whispered into her strawberry-scented pillow. *'Now it is time that I get my beauty sleep. A tired Princess is not of any use to anybody.'*

As the little Princess drifted into a troubled sleep, the Ziggercraft continued its descent. Nobody knew what to expect. Potatodai did his best to reassure all onboard that everything would be okay. 'If everybody sticks together and works like a team, everything will run like a dream,' he told them. Deep down, he was not half so confident, and he barely slept more than two hours at a time.

Several of his star friends winked and waved as they went by. *'Good luck,'* they echoed through the sky. *'We love you, Potatodai. Have a very safe journey. We will shine upon you as best we can. Give our love to the earthlings. Tell them that we will work extra hours to brighten up their nights if they are nice to you.'*

Two days went by, and then three, then four, and the Ziggercraft was still nowhere near Earth. The younger Zibazilians complained non-stop of boredom and lack of nice food.

'Let's play Binka Binka, the game of wits,' suggested Potatodai. *'When we finish that game, I will show you all how to play Zeg.'*

'We want to go home,' they moaned. *'We are all bored and all the nice food has been eaten.'*

To put a stop to this, Potatodai grabbed a few of the ringleaders and tied their wrists together with some sps floss, which was a string used for skipping. By tying them together, it meant that none of them could sit down and none of them could sleep, as there was not room for more than one in each of their wrinkle beds. Ten minutes later, the dishes sparkled, and the craft gleamed.

The journey was taking so long and Potatodai's mind began to gather bad thoughts. He wondered if Aza the star made up the whole story, and if the map was a fake. No! He should not think like that. After all, he had read about Planet Earth in one of his books, and the book, the star, the e-mail, Kaoisa and Old Man Time could not all be wrong. In addition to that, cherubs never told lies, so the directions must be real.

And then the moaning started again. *'Why should we take orders from you? You have already been banished from Zibazilia,'* chirped a dandelionblackberry with food all over his face. *'All you are allowed to do is play sentry.'*

'Yeah,' chorused a few brave hearts from the back. *'Who do you think you are?'*

Potatodai thought quickly. If he did not do something fast, there would be mutiny aboard the Ziggercraft and nobody would live to tell the tale.

However, luck was already on his side. At that exact moment, something very, very strange happened. It was the weirdest thing. An unexplained peace and happiness surrounded the Ziggercraft. Every single Zibazilian on board became silent and experienced a very happy feeling.

Each one went into their own little world and day dreamed of happy things. Even the Ziggercraft's engine purred with happiness, and zig-zagged with the same happiness over and back in the sky. Everybody said lovely things to each other. It was an amazing feeling. Then, just as fast as it happened, everything went back to normal again.

'What was that? I felt so happy and so cheerful,' gasped somebody.

'Me too,' said another voice. *'I have never felt so happy before.'*

'Look!' gasped somebody else, from a window seat. *'Look at the signpost in the sky. We have just passed through Dream Town. The sign says this is where the earthlings come when they daydream and when they want to think nice things. It helps them to relax, so the sign says. Oh, Aspalemon, do you think you could drive the Ziggercraft in there again? It was such a lovely place to be.'*

'Yes!' echoed everybody. *'Please can we go back to Dream Town?'*

Aspalemon the pilot was not listening. Tonight was night ten, which happened to be 31 October – Halloween night on Earth. He peered and peered through his telescope. If they had just passed through the earthlings' Dream Town then they must be close to Planet Earth. With a slightly lighter heart, he powered the

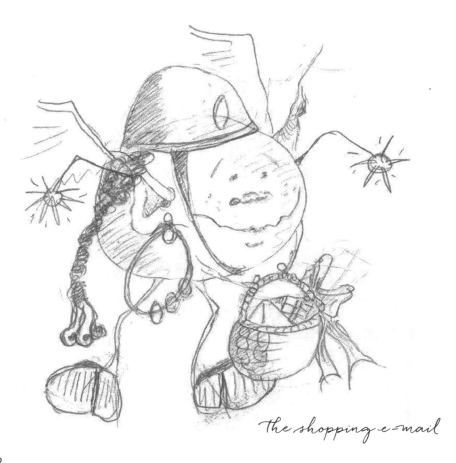

The shopping e-mail

Ziggercraft even faster downwards. *'Look, look down below!'* he shrieked. *'It can't be … yes, it can be … no, it can't be … yes, it is! It definitely is Planet Earth.'*

There was a stampede to the windows. Potatodai clenched his fists together, and wished and wished and wished with all his might that he were right. His tummy started to tingle with excitement. He had even dropped his plate of food on the ground, spilling some of it over the head of a tiny onionsycamorepea.

'Ouch! Watch what your doing, clumsy,' screamed the little onionsycamorepea, his voice suddenly getting lower when he realised that he had shouted at one of his elders.

'Oh, shut up,' Potatodai yelled back. *'We think we have spotted Planet Earth. That's far more important than a stupid dinner on your head.*

'Let's put our super-strength telescopes to use,' advised Potatodai. *'We must monitor what is going on down there before we even attempt to land. Can you all see the twinkling of zillions of lights down below?*

'Hooray!' shrieked Potatodai happily to whoever cared to listen. *'I really do believe it is Planet Earth. This is such great news. For a while, I thought we would never make it. It is now full steam ahead to Planet Earth.'*

Planet Earth took on a completely different picture from the eye of the telescope. It was nothing like what they would have imagined in their wildest dreams. There were millions and millions of earthling giants running here and there and everywhere. From the distance, they resembled giant ants. Some were small, and some were large.

Their homes looked like large boxes with funny things on top; some of the funny things had white powder pouring out of them. The earthlings moved from place to place in coloured machines with four round legs and two big eyes in front.

Potatodai was astonished. *'Their Ziggercrafts travel on the ground!'* he exclaimed. *'Wowee! Isn't that something? They must be smarter than we are! I am so jealous. Look, it is all so orderly. They drive on different sides of the road, so they will not crash. And, look, there are different coloured sticks with lights that tell them when to drive and when to stop.'*

'Look at all the water, with all the unusual brightly coloured things moving up and down from the bottom, and look at the water Ziggercrafts,' added Aspalemon.

'Planet Earth is made up of water and hundreds of different countries,' Potatodai proudly informed everybody. *'I have read that when it is daylight in one country, it is night time in another country.*

'But ... but, this is astonishing and so frightening. There are billions of these giants down there. The tallest one of us is nine inches in height. They will think that we are fruits and vegetables and plants!'

'Will we be eaten?' asked one lemonash in a state of panic. 'Should we turn around and go back now? I really do not feel like spending the rest of my life in the belly of an earthling. I would be so bored, and I would not have anyone to talk to in there.'

Aspalemon began to shout: 'Cool the chat, everybody. Potatodai, come here at once. I have very bad news for you.'

'What kind of news?' asked Potatodai nervously. 'What has happened, Aspalemon?'

'Nothing has happened yet,' answered Aspalemon, in a low tone. 'It is what could happen that scares me. Our supply of zonk is running very low.'

'But what about the spare tank we brought with us?' Potatodai asked.

Aspalemon threw a guilty look at Potatodai and stared out the window while speaking. 'The spare tank is not as big as it should be, because if we took anything bigger the craft would not be balanced properly. I have worked on the advice given by the bodyguards.'

'So, what's the story?' asked Potatodai, still not understanding fully what Aspalemon had to say. 'Please Aspa, do not tell me that we cannot go to Planet Earth. I could not live with the disappointment.'

Aspalemon shook his head. 'We are in really big trouble. The matter is very serious. I do beg of you to pay some attention.'

'What kind of trouble?' asked Potatodai innocently, suddenly aware of Aspalemon's raised and distraught tone. 'Are we going to be able to go to Earth or not? I beg you to answer my question now. Please stop beating about the bush.'

Aspalemon wiped a bead of perspiration from his forehead. 'Sadly, we will only be able to fly within fifty miles of Planet Earth and circle *around it for a short while. If we travel down the last fifty miles it will use up much more zonk. What if Earth could not supply us with a refill of zonk, and we were stranded down there forever and ever! Forty-five minutes is all the time we have for the downward part of the journey. That leaves us with just enough zonk to get us home.'*

'I told everybody that we should have made better preparations,' moaned Potatodai. *'Did anybody listen? Oh no, they did not. Turnipear and Carrotpeaash think they know everything but I know that their brains have gone for a long sleep. Anyway, now is not the time for complaining.*

'Look!' cried Potatodai, suddenly concentrating on Planet Earth again. *'Some of the earthlings have dinosaurs as pets. They have four legs and the Earth around them is all green. Is that a bag some of them have hanging underneath their bodies? I do believe it is, and look, there is an earthling taking liquid out of the bag and some of the dinosaurs are eating the ground. Look!'* he yelled again, with his eyes glued tightly to the telescope, *'this is all so exciting.'*

'We should have taken your advice,' agreed Aspalemon in a dull voice.

'Advice about what?' laughed Potatodai, who was still so excited over finding Planet Earth that he seemed to have forgotten everything Aspalemon had just told him.

'We should have planned this whole operation better,' admitted Aspalemon. *'You wanted Turnipear and Carrotpeaash and me to consult old Bewt from Planet Tilahita before we left. You said that he was old and wise and had a great interest in the history of planets. You said that he may have an idea of the length of the journey to Earth, but we were all too stubborn to listen to you. All we knew was the direction in which Planet Earth lay. Now we are in very big trouble.'*

Potatodai reassured Aspalemon as best he could: *'Aspalemon, don't be too hard on yourself. I blame Turnipear and Carrotpeaash. They were the ones who would not wait. They did not trust my judgement. They are jealous of me so my opinion, no matter how good it was, would not matter. They wanted to get all the credit for organising the trip.'*

Aspalemon wiped a bead of sweat from his forehead once again and then spoke. 'This whole matter is extremely serious. Within a short while, we will be using the spare tank of zonk fuel, which we brought as an emergency, and when that is gone, we will not be able to bring the Ziggercraft back to Zibazilia.

'As I already told you, if we don't leave here within forty-five minutes I cannot guarantee you all a safe passage home. If we run out of zonk even a few seconds from home, then we will just keep falling through the skies and we will all die. There may be no zonk on Earth,' Aspalemon warned again. *'These giants may use something else to fuel their Earth crafts.'*

'We can't turn back now,' wailed Potatodai, who was only now taking in the seriousness of the situation. *'We will have to take the chance that we will get zonk.'*

'And what if we don't?' asked Aspalemon. Most of the crew had now gathered at the cabin door to find out what was going on. One little pumpkinpea started crying. *'We are all going to die,'* he wailed. *'Let us go home now and forget about Planet Earth.'*

'Yes, let's do that,' echoed a few banana plums from the back. *'This was all such a stupid idea. We are bored and frightened. Please, Potatodai, let us go home to our own Planet. We are sorry for all the horrible things we said to you over the last few days.'*

Potatodai had a big lump in the back of his throat. His heart felt as if it had divided in two. *'What am I going to tell my little Princess?'*

he thought. *'How can I tell her that I let her down? It is all so near and yet so far.'*

Suddenly, a super brainwave entered his head. *'I will throw away the lucky stone which the bodyguards gave me and instead use the stone which Luna the moon gave me. It might bring me better luck.'*

Luna the moon had once given him a small, dark stone, which he told him would bring him luck. It was lucky that Potatodai had remembered to bring it. He clenched it between his hands and then placed the bodyguards' stone on the ground and stomped it to pieces.

'Help me, special Luna stone,' he pleaded as he squeezed it very, very tightly. *'Help us to get to Planet Earth and help us to get back home safely. I should never have accepted a special stone from Turnipear and Carrotpeaash when I knew I had you with me all the time.'*

Instantly, the stone worked, as seconds later a very loud rumbling noise filled the entire craft. Sparks began to pour from the left-hand engine of the Ziggercraft. Several of the crew were thrown from their seats. The Ziggercraft spluttered and coughed.

'Is it going to blow up?' cried a young lemontulip from the back. *'Are we all going to be killed?'*

'No, of course you are not,' assured Potatodai, hoping that he was telling him the truth. *'Everything is going to be alright. This is known as turbulence.'*

With great difficulty, Potatodai crept his way, on all fours, to the cockpit. Aspalemon had his head pressed against the cockpit window. He was mumbling quietly to himself.

'Its not turbulence,' he cried. *'A passing object has hit us. I am trying to balance the craft but there is a big weight on the side of it.*

Everybody, get your parachutes ready but don't do anything until I tell you.'

The craft continued to somersault in a very dangerous fashion and everybody's tummy felt very sick. *'Are we going to be stranded on Earth forever and ever? What happens if our parachute lands in the water? What if we all get separated?'*

The questions kept pouring from the back but Potatodai and Aspalemon were not listening. They were desperately trying to get the craft balanced again. This whole journey to Planet Earth was turning in to a very bad nightmare. Not only were they running out of zonk, but now this misfortune. *'Let's go back to earthling Dream Town,'* little voices echoed from time to time. *'Dream Town will make it all better. It was such a lovely few moments.'*

'Shut it you lot,' yelled Aspalemon. *'I cannot hear myself think. Shut it, you lot, I said!'*

'Look, look,' screamed a dandeliongrape from the back of the assembled audience, just as the Ziggercraft began to overbalance to the left. *'Look over there!'* Everybody turned in panic. *'There is a weird black thing hanging onto the window. And, it is making a really weird noise. Can you hear it?'*

'Hooky, Pooky, 'tis so spooky,' boomed the voice.

Then, as if by a miracle, the craft stopped somersaulting, and Potatodai slid the cabin window a tiny fraction open.

'Who's there?' he yelled in a nervous voice. *'Who's there? Tell us who you are this instant? We are not here to cause any trouble. We have come from Planet Zibazilia and are visiting Planet Earth. Princess Zamba sent us on this mission.'*

'Who art zeee?' boomed a loud, cackling voice. *'Hubble dubble bubble, get me out of this trooouble.'*

Potatodai and Aspalemon were terrified. Their hands shook with fear and perspiration rolled from their faces. The creature outside was the ugliest and scariest thing they had ever met. It had a long thin body, a long, carrot-like nose full of warts and spots and hair, and the ugliest face they had ever seen in their whole lives.

'Keep control of the Ziggercraft,' Potatodai yelled. *'I will deal with this.'*

'Are you an earthling?' he called out to the creature doing his very best to keep calm.

'Nooo!' it yelled back. *'Do not insulty me. I am a normal witch going about my normal business in the skyyy. My stick and cape are caught in your stupid machine. Who are you, anyway? You look like mixed-up fruits and veggies. Oooh, looky at you, you have a branch sticking out of your head. Steady the thing up until I get my stick and cape out, will you?'*

'How can we release your cape and stick; we can't get out of the craft! You will have to get in here with us, witch. At least then, the craft will balance. We will then try and free them,' roared Potatodai.

'Shall we take a chance?' asked Aspalemon.

Potatodai was willing to try anything at this crucial stage. *'Yes,'* he answered. *'We have enough crew members to overpower it, if it causes any trouble. Silence, everybody!'* roared Potatodai, as the ugly creature clambered in through the window.

Both parties stood staring at each other for at least a minute. Apart from being ugly, the witch reeked of weird smells. When it lifted its hand, it smelt of one smell and when it blinked, it smelt of a completely different spell.

'I'm a witch,' it cackled. *'How many more times do I have to tell you? So would you ever dooo me a favour and stop squinting your silly*

little eyes at me. Well, to tell the real truth, I am a junior woman witch. I am still training. I am only allowed to have a few magic spells until I qualify.

'My name is Snizzlezallig, and I live down here in the sky with lots of other witches. And where do you crazy beautiful fruit come from?' she asked. *'I haven't seen you around the sky before.'*

'We're from Planet Zibazilia,' shouted a brave kiwimelonsycamore from the back. *'And, if you don't mind, please stop calling us fruit. We're not crazy either,'* he added bravely. *'We are called Zibazilians.'*

All the juniors giggled, obviously quite impressed with his brave outburst.

Egged on by the giggles, he continued: *'Have you ever heard of Zibazilia? I bet you have not. It's the best Planet in the whole universe.'*

'It is the best,' echoed his followers, now beginning to enjoy the strange happenings.

Snizzlezallig was so intrigued that she began to wiggle her chin around and around in a clockwise manner and then in an anti-clockwise manner. *'Well, if you lot say you don't look like fruit then I must look like a nellyphant,'* she giggled. *'I've never seen anything like you before. You smell delicious and you look delicious – almost good enough to eat.*

'Hey! You over there, you look like a banana with a pea on your head. Do you lot come around here often? I'd say you don't, 'cause me and my buddies are around the sky every night and we would have spotted you before.

'Hey you, spokesman! I think you are quite cute,' she cooed as she gazed admiringly at Potatodai. *'You look like a potato mixed up with a daisy.*

'Are you old? Your skin looks a bit withered but you still look gooorgeous if I may say so and you do smell ever so nice. You smell like our roasty Sunday taties.'

'Stop wasting precious time,' hissed Aspalemon into Potatodai's ear. *'This is a panic situation. Ask her advice about Earth and then tell her our zonk is running out. If we land, we may get no zonk! Do I have to remind you again?'* he yelled in a frustrated tone. *'If that happens we will be stuck down there forever.'*

'We're all going to die, we're all going to die,' wailed the crew, who had overheard him. Aspalemon's advice had started to make sense but was it too late. They had to think and think very fast. Their precious time and fuel were slipping away very, very quickly. Should they turn and go back and give up the chance of ever visiting Planet Earth, or did they take a chance and go there? Now, this witch creature had caught her cape and wand in their Ziggercraft. It was all becoming too much to handle.

'What d'ya want me to do, fruity babes?' Snizzlezallig asked, sensing their distress. *'I must be in a good mood tonight to offer to help you lot, especially after you causing damage to my wand and my cape. That beautiful fruity smell must have gone to my brain.*

'I still haven't heard how you are going to release me. My coaty woaty and my sticky wicky are stuck in the side of your spacecraft.'

'Please,' pleaded Potatodai and Aspalemon together, *'dear kind witch, please find a way to get us out of this mess. We will be forever in your debt.'* Snizzlezallig smiled. *'You lot forever in my debt! Hmm! I hope you're listening to that, spud.'* Potatodai pretended not to hear. He would agree to almost anything to sort out this terrible mess.

'Well, let me see now,' cackled Snizzlezallig. *'I hope you lot realise that it is Halloween down on Earth tonight and it is the only time witches are welcome down there. All I want is my wand and my cape,*

because I need to practise my spell. I am not sure how I can help you lot.

'Even if I was a fully qualified witchy, I would not be able to perform any magic powers up this high in the sky. We witches can only perform magic powers when we get within a few miles of Earth, and only on certain days of the year. So, you fruities, I cannot help you this high in the sky even if I wanted to. Understand?'

Everybody groaned. *'Think of something,'* they begged.

Snizzlezallig thought long and hard and then her gaze drifted towards Potatodai. *'There is one thing,'* she cackled. *'Even though I am not supposed to carry passengers, I can take that potato cutie on the back of my broomstick to Planet Earth, that is, if I get my stick free. You lot are so lucky that it is Halloween night, otherwise the earthlings would think we had gone soft if they saw us witchies on any other day down there. The sky is our home and only on special occasions do we go anywhere else.'*

'But what about the others?' asked Potatodai, still hardly able to take in all that was happening. *'You say you will take me to Earth, witch. But … but …'* he stammered nervously, *'what about the others? How are they going to get to Planet Earth, and what about our Ziggercraft?'*

'Yes, witch,' echoed everybody. *'What about the rest of us? We want to go to Planet Earth too.'*

'How biggy do you thinky I am?' snarled Snizzlezallig. *'Do you thinky I have the back of a nellyphant? Or do you thinky I have the humpies of a camel?'*

Aspalemon decided to interrupt. *'Potatodai, we will wait here for you, but time is against us. All we have now is approximately thirty-five minutes. If you are longer than that, we will have to return to Zibazilia. I am now warning you. While we circle around up here, I will only use one of the engines. That will help to save some zonk. But, remember you have thirty-five minutes, not one minute more. We wish you well on your journey, and we hope you come back with some very interesting information.'*

'What about us?' wailed an auberginetomatowillow, nervously sucking the juices from his bat-leg drink. *'Don't we get a chance to visit Planet Earth? I'm tired and fed up being cooped up here for days and days.'* Nobody was listening to a word he said.

Without any further hesitation, Potatodai decided that he would take the chance. On a number of occasions he asked himself if he'd gone mad. He was putting his fate in the hands of a witch, a sky creature he had never laid eyes on before.

This funny-looking, smelly witch might take him anywhere and hold him to ransom, but he was willing to take the chance. Underneath her ugliness, she had a kind look, and somewhere in his head, he felt he could trust her. He was willing to do anything to bring a smile to the face of dear, sweet, Princess Zamba of Zibazilia. He was prepared to die if he had to.

But suddenly yet another problem entered Potatodai's head: *'And if I do go with you, witch, how are we going to free your wand and your cape? They are lodged firmly in the engine of our Ziggercraft. We will not be able to free them unless we land somewhere, and we cannot do that.'*

'Why did we not think of that first?' Aspalemon exhaled. *'Do something,'* he warned. *'Do something urgently. The zonk and our time are running out fast. Think, think, and think!'*

'Do something,' echoed the young Zibazilians from the back of the craft. *'Time is ticking away really fast.'*

'I suppose that you lot are leaving this up to me to sort out,' cackled Snizzlezallig as she bent her head out of the window, tensed up her muscles, and went into a very, very deep trance. Her beady eyes began to bulge out of her forehead and her nose looked as if it was getting longer. Then a very smelly purple liquid seeped out from under her wrinkled skin.

'Her witchy underwear must be dirty,' mocked a voice from a windowseat.

'Shh!' replied almost everybody else. *'This is the last chance we have. It is not the right time for jokes.'*

'Sorry, everybody,' said the little voice. *'I was just playing happy, even though I am sad.'*

Potatodai was fascinated. *'What on earth are you doing, witch? You look as if you are in pain.'*

Snizzlezallig had her face scrunched up into a tight ball.

'Don't make me think you have no brains,' Snizzlezallig cackled. *'Surely you can work out what I am doing. How do you expect me to get my cape and my stick out of the engine without getting help, and you lot haven't a clue how to help me? I have to sendy my witchy scent out to a witchy friend.'*

Potatodai was even more intrigued. *'So, what will your friend do?'* he asked. Before he had time to blink, a whirring sound in the sky distracted them, and another weird smell filled the air. This smell was even stinkier than the last one.

'Gizo, Gizooo! I knew you would come to rescue me,' beamed Snizzlezallig. *'I have got myself into a pickle and I want you to help.'*

Suddenly a thunderous noise boomed all around, and a large flash of orange and blue light whizzed through the sky. The other witch who appeared on the scene looked smaller but a little older. One of her nostrils was covered in fur and the other was covered in matted hair. She had no warts.

'Where did you find that cutie pie?' she hissed, staring at Potatodai, who at this time was balancing himself at the door of the

Ziggercraft. *'Methinks he looky like a cutie potato and look at his daisy eyes.'*

'Mind your own business, Gizo,' snapped Snizzlezallig. *'Just free my wand and cape now, as I need to take this potato to Earth. Stop staring! I found him first.'*

Gizo tugged and tugged and tugged, and finally Snizzlezallig was free again.

'Got to go now,' Gizo cackled. *'Glad to be of help to a friend. Tell me all the gossip later. Toodle pip, dearie. Maybe I will see you down on Earth later this evening. Should be a fun night; I'm dying to try out my new spells.'*

'Tanky 'anky, Gizo,' roared Snizzlezallig, as Gizo disappeared into the night sky.

Snizzlezallig looked Potatodai up and down. *'Bring a coaty woaty – or in your case a skinny winny – with you, potato cutie, that is if you own such a thing. It is going to be a cold spin down to Earth. Broomsticks have no roofs and they go at amazing speed. Count yourself honoured, spud, to have the priviledge of travelling on my broomstick. I will be in terrible trouble if this is found out.'*

'And be back in less than thirty-three minutes, or otherwise we will have to leave without you,' yelled Aspalemon. *'Do not leave it a minute longer. I have done my calculations and that is the very most time we can wait.'*

'Good luck, Potatodai,' roared the gang. *'Good luck!'*

Sitting on a broomstick was a very chilly experience, as Potatodai soon found out. *'Wheeeeeee,'* squealed Snizzlezallig, as Potatodai hung on to her black cloak for dear life. *'Isn't this fun, me and a spuddy on our way to Earthy.'*

'Snizzlezallig, could I ask you a big favour?' yelled Potatodai. *'Will you wait for me down on Earth and take me back before the Ziggercraft leaves?'*

Snizzlezallig giggled: *'You be nice to me spud and your wish will be my command.'*

'What, what do you want me to do for you?' asked Potatodai nervously. *'How would you like me to be nice to you?'*

Snizzlezallig scrunched her witchy face up into a ball. *'Don't you worry,'* she cooed. *'I will find something. Down, down, down we go, zibby dibby yibby. Tiggly wiggly, vroom vroom, vroooom. I hope we don't bang into any of those stupid e-mails or we're in big trouble.'*

Potatodai was intrigued. *'E-mails?'* he gasped. *'What are e-mails?'*

'Stoppy all the questions, spud. I will explain later. Do you want to get to Earth or don't you? If you dooo, allow me to do the talking and you keep your little spud mouth closed. Do you follow, spud? Ouchy pouchy, here come a gang of e-mails; duck, spud, or we will be knocked off the broomstick. Duck I tell you, quick!'

Potatodai ducked just in the nick of time. *'Please,'* he begged, *'please tell me about those e-mail things. I am asking for a particular reason.*

What are they, and why are they flying up and down to Earth? Why are they all carrying envelopes? Are they visitors? Why are there so many?'

Snizzlezallig threw him a confused look. *'And what's the reason for all your questions?'* she asked.

'It's just that I thought I heard our Princess saying that one of them had come to visit her a few days ago.'

'Nonsense,' sneered Snizzlezallig. *'Those e-mails are not allowed to visit planets that high up in the sky. They only bounce off the top of the sky and bounce back down to their destination. What kind of a stupid backward planet do you live on, spud? You seem to know nothing about nothing.'*

'That's not true,' argued Potatodai. *'There are loads of things going on in Planet Zibazilia that you and the earthlings know nothing about. Am I correct in saying that you never even heard of our planet?'*

'Shutty gobby, spuddy,' Snizzlezallig yelled. 'I have to concentrate on my journey.'

It was all such an exciting adventure, that Potatodai decided not to get into an argument. The worst thing that could possibly happen was that this ugly witch would start arguing with him and that she would refuse to bring him back to the waiting Ziggercraft. He was very aware that time definitely was not on his side.

It was time to make some nice conversation. *'It must be very difficult for you to guide that broomstick through the planes and those e-mails and everything. I think you are so clever. You must have loads of brains!'*

It worked. Snizzlezallig threw her head back and smiled proudly. *'I know all the shortcuts, spud. You can rely on me.'* For a split second, her ugly face showed a tiny beam of a smile and a large black tooth stuck out from the side of her mouth. It had a piece missing.

'I don't travel the skies all night without knowing something, do I? I might look stupid, spuddy, but I am not. Not long now and we will be landing on Planet Earth. Spend the few minutes on Earth wisely, as you do not have long. I will drop you somewhere dark and quiet, where there all the earthlings are indoors.'

Potatodai breathed a deep sigh of relief. It was obvious that his attempt at nice chat had paid off; it looked like the smelly, scruffy witch was now on his side.

As they came closer to Earth, the sky became very congested. Potatodai was so intrigued by the planes, birds, and those weird e-mail things, that he forgot how nervous he really was about his visit to this ever so strange planet.

'Wheeeeeee!' shouted Snizzlezallig, excitedly. *'Hold tight. We are about to land.'* Earth was now only a few seconds away. Potatodai's heart began to beat faster and faster and faster. Everything was now so much larger. He could see that the witch was looking for a place to park her broomstick. His stomach was in knots; half of it was fright and the other half was airsickness.

They were circling over rows and rows of the box things, or houses, as she called them. Potatodai shivered and was unable to speak with the fright.

'Why are you shaking, spud?' Snizzlezallig asked. *'Are you scared? Earthlings are okey dokey. They never did anything to me. They will be scared of you too, so do not fret.'*

'But I am so little and they are so large,' confessed Potatodai, in a voice that quivered. 'And they eat fruit and veggies. I look like a

potato and a daisy mixed up, so they could gobble me up and spit me out.'

'Do you want to be dropped or don't you?' grumbled Snizzlezallig. *'By the time I have dropped you back to your craft I will have to have my tea and go down to Earthy again, and, as, I told you already, it's Halloween time. We don't have much time. Do you have any brains or do you just not listen to your elders?*

'Ouchy pouchy, get out of my way you stupid e- mail,' Snizzlezallig yelled as one whisked past her, almost knocking the hat from her head. *'You lot think you own the sky,'* she roared, but the e-mail did not even bother to look back. It was obvious that the e-mails were used to witches moaning.

'That's one of the deleted ones,' Snizzlezallig explained. *'When they get deleted they become very bitter and try to make everyone's life a misery. They tear up and down the sky and fight with everybody else. Earthlings delete e-mails that carry bad information or information that they do not need anymore. I really wish those earthlings would stop sending each other those stupid e-mail messages. The sky is a mess.'*

Finally, after what seemed like an age, Snizzlezallig landed on top of a chimney. It was dark on this section of Planet Earth, so most of the earthlings were indoors. *'Get away from the chimney smoke, spud,'* she yelled. *'That stuff could choke you, and makey sure you don't fall down the chimney. If you dooooo, you will be a black sooty spud.*

'Now you beautiful thingy, I have done just as you requested. Never say a witchy does not keep her promises! You wanted to get to Earth and I brought you to Earth. I will be back at this very spot again in thirty minutes. Be ready. You heard what your people said. One minute late and they will go without you.'

'Thank you, witch – er, I mean Snizzle,' whispered Potatodai nervously. *'I am forever in your debt for what you have done for me and for my Princess, and for the people of Planet Zibazilia.'*

'Well if you are, then give me a kissy wissy before you leave, spud.'

'Give you a what?' asked Potatodai, the eyes popping out of his face with shock.

'Will you give e a kissy?' asked Snizzlezallig. *'I really fancy you.'*

Potatodai stared blankly at her. *'How do I give you a kissy? I have not got the faintest clue how to do that!'* he confessed. *'Do witches and earthlings carry kissies with them to hand out?'*

'Forget it!' sneered Snizzlezallig. *'I keep forgetting that you come from a backward planet. Imagine you aliens do not even know how to kissy.'*

Seconds later, the ugly witch disappeared into the night sky and Potatodai found himself all alone. He carefully slid halfway down the drainpipe of a large house. These earthlings had their house painted a dreadful shade of green.

Cautiously, he peered through the window. A giant woman earthling was stirring something in a big pot. A giant man earthling was staring at a box. He was eating brown things and there were loads of apples in a dish on the table.

'Oh no,' thought Potatodai in great horror. 'We have living fruit like that up in Zibazilia. That earthling would gobble us up too!'

The picture on the box the man was watching showed earthlings kicking something white and round.

Potatodai crept across to the next window. A smaller earthling was looking out the window of his bedroom. He looked very sad and very bored. He was sitting in a very funny-looking chair with wheels. The window was slightly open; Potatodai decided to be brave and he stuck his nose under it.

'How do you do, earthling,' he chirped in his loudest and politest voice. 'My name is Potatodai. I come from Planet Zibazilia, a planet way up at the top of the sky. This is my first time on Earth and I am only here on a very short visit. What is your name?'

The little boy earthling's eyes shone with wonder. 'I can't believe it!' he shrieked. 'I have never seen anything like you in my whole life. I must be dreaming, or else a witch has put a spell on me because it's Halloween night. Maybe I fell asleep in my wheelchair. You look like a big potato with daisies and roots sticking out all over you! Are you really from another planet? Then again, you have to be, don't you, because otherwise you wouldn't look so weird.'

'Yes, I am,' answered Potatodai. 'As I just said, this is the first time we Zibazilians have been to Planet Earth. Our Ziggercraft is running out of zonk so I can only stay for a very short while.

The little boy smiled, and the sad expression disappeared from his face. 'Hiya,' he whispered gently. 'I'm Jason, and I'm ten years of age. I can't believe this … I just can't believe this is happening,' he repeated. 'I'm really not sure whether I should be scared or honoured to meet an alien. I always thought that aliens were make-believe. I can't decide if I should call my Mom and Dad either.'

'Don't do that, little earthling,' begged Potatodai. 'Please let us chat first.'

'Sure, alien,' said Jason. After all, it was Halloween evening, and weird things were meant to happen on Halloween. Why bring his parents in now and spoil all the fun?

'Please may I come in?' asked Potatodai? 'I am cold, tired, and a little frightened. Princess Zamba sent me down here on a special mission to find out all about you earthlings. Did you know, little earthling, that seeds blew up from your planet into space hundreds of years ago? Did you know that the seeds got all mixed up and had babies, and here we are?'

'Really!' Jason gasped in astonishment.

'May I ask please if you are a baby earthling?' Potatodai asked Jason. 'You are much smaller than the two in the next room.'

Jason smiled. 'I am their son, but I'm also different than most earthlings.'

'You are, are you?' asked Potatodai. 'Why? Have they stolen you from a different planet? If they have, then I will ask Old Man Time where you came from and we will have you returned.'

'Nothing like that,' explained Jason. *'There is something wrong with my legs. Because of that, I have to sit in this stupid wheelchair from day to day. All my friends can play ball and go horse riding. All I can do is sit and watch.*

'When I finish school every evening, I play games on my computer. Then my mum leaves the curtains open and I stare up at the moon and the stars before I fall asleep. They are my friends and I tell them all my secrets. They never laugh or jeer at me like some of the kids at school.'

Potatodai did his best to hide a rather large tear, which had formed in the corner of his eye. He didn't want earthlings to think that the people of Planet Zibazilia were crybabies.

'Then it was luck that I found you, wasn't it?' he whispered gently, still feeling ever so sorry for this little earthling. *'You can now boast to your friends that you met somebody from Planet Zibazilia. I was meant to find you. I just know I was.'*

'My friends won't believe me,' Jason replied. *'None of us have ever heard of Planet Zibazilia. Why not stick around for a while; you can come to school with me on Friday. We get a half day on Friday and I could introduce you to everybody!'*

Potatodai wished with all his heart he could. *'I can't, I already told you. Our Ziggercraft is running short of zonk, and we are afraid to bring the craft down here.'*

'We don't have any zonk down here,' said Jason, half guessing that his new friend was talking about fuel. *'We only have petrol and diesel, and I don't know if they are the same. I can ask my dad for you if you wish. I will tell him I am doing a project for school about aliens.'*

'No, no, no!' gasped Potatodai, feeling terribly uneasy at the thought of meeting a giant earthling. He liked this little earthling, but he did not want his dad messing things up, as time was

running out fast. He also did not want to run the risk of getting himself kidnapped and never going home.

Somewhere deep down in his heart he wished that there was something he could do to brighten up the life of his new earthling friend before he departed. Maybe he should whisk him off to Planet Zibazilia to meet his Princess? But looking at Jason, Potatodai was aware that he would not fit into the Ziggercraft. Anyway, it would be cruel to separate him from his parents. He would just have to find out as much as he could for the remainder of his visit. *'How can I do that?'* he thought. *'I only have a few minutes left. This is all so unfair.'*

'Sit on my bed, alien. Please, please, please,' begged Jason. *'This is where I sleep. Please lie on my pillow and I can always say that an alien slept on my bed, even if nobody believes me. I can dream about you, up there in the sky. I can wave to you at night, even though I know you won't be able to see me.'*

Potatodai crept down from the windowsill. He was completely fascinated by Jason's bed. *'Oh my golly gosh,'* he gasped. *'It's about a hundred times the size of our hammocks. All of us Zibazilians could nearly fit in this bed. Oh! It is so comfy. I want to lie here for hours and hours. I'm so sleepy.'*

Seconds later, Jason heard a very loud snore and was astonished to find that his visitor had fallen into a very deep sleep. Little puffs of steam gushed from his tiny nose and he made a gurgling sound. His tiny face was hot and he smelt of chips. Jason was tempted to call his mum and dad and show them this potato covered in daisies, asleep on his pillow. Then again, it would be ever so nice to have a secret. It would be nice to know something that nobody else knew.

He wondered if he should wake his new friend. He did say he only had a few minutes. But his visitor had travelled millions of miles, so Jason decided to let him sleep for just a little while. He was obviously very tired. Jason searched the sky with his eyes in the hope ofcatching a glimpse of the alien's spacecraft, but it was nowhere to be seen.

'What have I done?' Potatodai howled, as he awoke with a start. 'How could I have fallen asleep? How could I have been so stupid? Why did you not waken me, little earthling?'

Jason did his best to calm his visitor. 'You are not stupid and I am so pleased that you paid me a visit. I also love that you slept in my bed and that you found it so comfortable. Will you come down and see me again sometime? This has been the best day of my life. Just give me the questions that you need answered and the next time you call, I will have the answers all written out for you.'

'I would be honoured to call again,' beamed Potatodai. 'Right now, I do have to go. I am hoping that I will get back safely and on time to my waiting craft. I will do my best to come to Earth again soon. I am so very pleased to have met you. Could I take something with me to make sure my Princess believes that I met an earthling?'

Jason was only too delighted. 'Take my woolly hat and, here, take some roasted peanuts … yuck! What is that funny smell? It smells like incense sticks.'

'Well, ah, um … I'm not sure,' lied Potatodai. He had instantly recognised the scent of Snizzlezallig the witch and was so relieved that she had come back to bring him to the Ziggercraft. But he was also very disappointed that the information he had taken from Planet Earth was so little.

'Psst! Over here,' hissed Snizzlezallig. 'I know its Halloween, but dooooon't let that little boy see me. He has had enough shocks for one day. Hurry up, spuddy, your craft will be leaving in a few minutes.'

Potatodai jumped onto the windowsill. *'Toodle pip, earthling Jason, I will explain everything the next time I call, I promise. I'm so sorry I do not have a pressie for you. Things did not go according to plan, but we will see each other again soon. It was a great pleasure to meet you.'*

'Please come back soon,' urged Jason. *'This is the most exciting thing that has ever happened in my entire life.'*

Potatodai promised with all his heart that he would come back for another visit, but in the back of his mind he wondered how he was going to do it. He would think of something. After all, he always did.

Yes, Planet Earth was a very intriguing place and he was determined to find out more about it. He had also made a promise to a little earthling and Potatodai never, ever broke his promises.

'Goodbye!' he shouted, ignoring Jason's question about how he was getting back to his spaceship.

Snizzlezallig's long nose wobbled from side to side as she balanced her broomstick. *'We only have a few minutes,'* she hissed. *'Sometimes it takes a while to pick up speed when I leave Planet Earthy. Hold on tighty, spuddy, we are about to take off.'*

Up, up, up they sped, narrowly missing all the traffic in the sky.

'Can you see the lights of the Ziggercraft yet?' Potatodai asked again and again, but Snizzlezallig just shook her head. The airometer on her wand told her they had reached fifty miles, but they could not catch any glimpse of the Ziggercraft.

'This is where I collected you, spud,' she said, quite puzzled. *'It was at this very spot. My wand has a compass and an airometer on it, that's why I'm sooooo sure.'* Snizzlezallig circled the patch of sky three times but there was no Ziggercraft.

'Try another direction,' roared Potatodai, who was now in a frenzy. *'You must have gone the wrong way, you silly witch. You probably cannot see because of those big warts on your nose. And look, one of your eyebrows has half covered your eye.'*

Snizzlezallig ignored his nasty remark. She was aware that her Zibazilian spud was in a terrible state. She assured him that she knew the sky like the back of her hand, and there was no way she had gone the wrong way.

'What has gone wrong? Why have they left?' cried Potatodai, realising the witch was telling the truth and that he was in the most awful and terrible predicament.

'*Their fuel supply must have been less than they thought, and they had to depart,*' mused Snizzlezallig.

Potatodai stomach started to churn as the terrible truth began to dawn on him.

'*But we were here exactly on time. Does that mean that … that … I am stranded down here?*' he asked, suddenly feeling ever so scared. '*Does it mean that I will never see my planet and my beloved Princess again? I do not even have a way of contacting her.*'

Snizzlezallig wore a very sly look on her face and remained very silent.

Zaka, a senior brusselsycamore page, first heard the hum of the Ziggercraft as it approached Planet Zibazilia. He expressed a sigh of relief that he had remembered to wash his ears that morning. He knew how important any kind of information was to his Princess.

He could see Glitterati and his staff of stars guiding the craft carefully back to its home. Each star tilted forward its corners as the craft passed, in recognition of its wonderful achievement. With great haste, Zaka alerted the second senior page on duty, and he, in turn, quickly told the Princess.

'Zope! Zope!' squealed the Princess. *'Help me to get ready and make sure I look very pretty. I do not have very much time. Today is a very, very important day. It is possible that Potatodai and Aspalemon will have brought an earthling with them!*

'I do hope that Turnipear and Carrotpeaash are out there about to give them a big welcome. In fact, they may be disembarking from the Ziggercraft as we speak. If there is an earthling on board, we must give him a very good impression of our planet from the moment he steps off the craft.'

The little page was rather mystified. *'But, Your Royal Highness,'* he ventured, *'the tallest of our people are only nine inches high. How could one of those earthling giants fit into our palace? In fact, it would also be impossible to carry one in our Ziggercraft, unless their legs hung out the windows.'*

The Princess smiled. *'Do not fear, my little helper,'* she beamed. *'My trusted bodyguards have been thinking ahead. They are ready at all times to blow up a large tent at the side of the palace. I am so looking forward to meeting Potatodai and hearing all about his trip. Go at once and prepare the weary travellers a banquet so fine that we will be the envy of all the other planets. Bring the most exquisite gnat juice and the claws from the largest bats. Have every member of the kitchen staff on standby. Hey, hey! Before you go, brush my hair and tell me I look good.'*

'*You look adorable, Your Royal Highness,*' the little page reassured her. '*The earthling will be so impressed by you.*'

Princess Zamba giggled and gave one last look in the mirror. '*Gilly golly gosh,*' she whooped. '*I am about to meet one of my ancestors. I hope he will like us. Then again, it is my place as Princess of Zibazilia to make sure he is happy here. I hope none of my people have let me down with our arrangements!*'

The little Princess made herself comfortable in her favourite golden chair. At least a dozen times, she shook her foot, flicked open the tiny mirror tied onto her shoe and examined herself from head to toe, and from toe to head, just to make sure she was looking good – even better than good. Her gold tiara glistened in the light. She beamed with happiness and excitement.

Zope kept running in and out of her chambers with the latest news. It seemed like ages since she had received word that they were approaching. Finally, he charged in with the news that she had waited so eagerly to hear. '*They have landed,*' he beamed. '*The craft has finally landed, Your Highness.*'

Zaka gave him a thump from behind. '*Shut it,*' he mumbled. '*You are exciting the Princess too much. Wait until everybody gets out of the Ziggercraft before you give her any more news. She will be heartbroken if the news is bad. Look, it's Aspalemon the pilot and he is coming this way.*'

In the distance, the onlookers could see Carrotpeaash and Turnipear racing out to lead him to the Princess. The rest of the crew stood beside the craft.

'*Yazza zazza!*' squealed Princess Zamba. '*Quick, Zope! Pull up a special chair for Aspalemon. I want him to sit beside me in a seat of honour. I want another special seat for my dear friend Potatodai.*'

'*Will … will that be necessary, Your Highness?*' asked Zope, who had seen the terrible look of despair on Aspalemon's face. He could also see that Potatodai was not with the crew.

Aspalemon's face was indeed a picture of misery as he made his way sheepishly to where the Princess was sitting. She suddenly sensed that something was very wrong. Her pink strawberry skin grew very pale and her eyelashes began to tremble.

'*It's okay, Aspalemon, it's okay,*' she comforted him. '*I can see something terrible has happened. Tell me,*' she whispered calmly, '*tell me Aspa, what has happened? Why has Potatodai not come here to help you tell your tale? Bodyguards, have you barred him from coming to see me?*'

Both bodyguards shook their heads.

'*Then where is he?*' asked the Princess. '*Where is my good and loyal friend and sentry Potatodai?*'

Aspalemon answered in a very low voice. '*He went on a witch's broomstick to Planet Earth, but he did not come back quickly enough so we had to leave without him. We did not have any choice. I misjudged the amount of zonk we had left in the tank and I had to leave a few moments earlier than I thought I would.*'

'*And how do you propose to get him back?*' asked Carrotpeaash in an angry tone.

'We don't know. We will do our best to come up with something, but we haven't thought of anything yet.'

'Let's leave the feast for another time,' mumbled the tearful Princess. *'How could we celebrate when one of our own is missing? When we may never see them again?'* Everybody agreed, and they all filed out in turn. Dark black curtains came down over the windows of Zibazilia Palace that night.

The inflatable tent was packed away in silence. Turnipear and Carrotpeaash prepared all kinds of treats for the Princess but she refused to eat or drink a single thing. It was a very sad night indeed.

It only took a few minutes to get to the witches' den. Before they had even arrived, a very strange smell had crept its way into Potatodai's nose. His potato skin began to tighten with fear. He was at the mercy of this ugly witch and there was not one thing he could do. All he could do was try to smile and keep calm.

The den proved to be creepier than creepy. It resembled a giant cobweb with a roof, made of fur, and it was suspended in the middle of the sky.

'How does it stay in the one place?' asked Potatodai, quite dumbfounded.

Snizzlezallig was not in the mood for talking. *'Shut it, spuddy, you have already upsetty all my plans for Halloween night. Just shutty gobby. I needy time to thinky.'*

They made their way through the opening of the witches' den, where Gizo sat on a rickety-looking seat, mending a broom. *'I'll tell you why our den stays in one place,'* she cackled. *'Oh, by the way, it's goody to see you again, alien. You are having a weird kind of day. Snizz, how did you manage to snare that gorgeous spud and get him back here?'*

Snizzlezallig was not in talking mood. *'Shut it, Gizo, and keep your handy dandys off my spud. Any questions that need answering will be done by me.'*

Potatodai was quick to intervene, having already sensed a rift between Gizo and Snizzlezallig. *'It all right, everybody, I do not need to know about your den. All I want is for your witches to find a way for me to get back to my planet and my lovely Princess. My Ziggercraft has left without me.'*

'Don't worry, spud, we will look after you,' cackled Gizo. *'Now let me tell you about our den.'*

'If you insist,' answered Potatodai, in a very deflated voice.

Gizo pulled her hat back from over her eyes. *'In each witch's den, spud, there is a senior witch, and she always has one magic spell which can last forever and ever. In the summer, she makes our den into a cobweb and in the winter, it changes to a nest made of fur. In fact, the weather is getting cold now so it's just about to turn into fur.'*
'

'Thanks for the explanation,' mumbled Potatodai, who was now fully aware of the large group of witches who were peering under the brim of their hats at him. It was the spookiest sight he had ever seen.

They mumbled, muttered, and cursed together but he could not understand one single word that they said. Gizo and Snizzlezallig stood to one side, wondering who was going to make the first move.

Potatodai counted twelve, no, thirteen witches, all dressed in black, who continued to mumble and mutter. From time to time one would spit into a giant dirty black pot. It was in this very pot, Gizo told him, that all the magic spells were made. Gizo explained that it takes six weeks and three days to make a new spell. And, if the spell is not used more than twelve times in each witch's calendar year, then it just becomes useless and will not work anymore.

Snizzlezallig moved forward. *'That's not true, Gizo. It takes six weeks and five days to make a new spell. Get your witchy facts right before you speak!'*

It was obvious to Potatodai that a rift was developing between Gizo and her friend Snizzlezallig. He could see Snizzlezallig pacing up and down, and twisting the tail of her cape into knots.

'I saw him fiiirst!' yelled Snizzlezallig.

'You may have spotted him first, but only for meee you would never have been rescued out of that spacecraft!' roared Gizo.

Potatodai was flattered. It was the first time in his whole life that two ladies fought over him. But then he privately asked himself if they could really be called ladies. Ladies were beautiful and dignified, but these witches were smelly and ugly. But before Potatodai had time to decide, something much more sinister happened.

Some of the elder witches had left their seats and were making their way towards him, their cloaks rustled as they approached.

'Oh no,' Potatodai thought. *'What am I going to do? I am at their mercy.'*

Unknown to Potatodai, Rittop, Suz, Jiop and a number of other elder witches had decided to have some fun and play a game. They had heard enough of the squabbling between Gizo and Snizzlezallig, and had decided to put an end to it. One of them waved a rather large, crooked wand and mumbled a long, complicated phrase.

Suddenly a large red football appeared, and a witch kicked it up in the air. When the football came down, they all put their spiky hats together and tried to pierce it. *'He won't have any brains by the time we have finished with him,'* one of them giggled. *'None of our flirty witches will want to date a dumb-dumb nerd.'*

Snizzlezallig felt the blood go from her face. *'What have you dooone, oh elders?'* she asked in a timid voice. *'Have you turned my guest into a football?'*

'Okay, okay,' giggled Rittop, the tall lanky witch, when she realised how angry Snizzlezallig was. *'We will return him to normal.'*

Once again, the assembled witches mumbled their spell and there was a low, hissing sound. Potatodai found himself lying on the floor. His head was spinning and it felt ever so sore.

'Sooorry,' cooed Gizo. *'It was kind of my fault that they turned you into a football. They were fed up with me and Snizzle fighting over you.'*

Snizzlezallig immediately launched into an attack. *'So you admit it was yooour fault, do you? You are such a jealous witch. You want everything for yourself.'*

Gizo flew into an immediate rage and tore the hat from Snizzlezallig's head.

'Stop it, you twooo,' yelled the senior witches together. *'We are in the process of making new spells and you are upsetting our concentration. This time you will be sorry,'* they roared and they immediately cast another spell.

Suddenly, and without any warning, Potatodai felt his head getting a little woozy, and then a lot woozier. He looked down at his feet and saw that there were four feet there instead of two. He felt his body getting smaller and lighter. And then, to make matters ten times worse, he lifted his leg and made his wee-wee against the side of the big black pot.

'What have you witches done this time?' yelled Gizo and Snizzlezallig together.

A witch with a crinkly, croaky voice answered, *'By changing this spud thing into a rat, none of you will fight over him. We know that you're both scared of rats, so he will continue to scurry around the place until you both stop fighting.'*

Snizzlezallig was furious. *'You can't dooo that, Rittop!'* she screamed. *'I promised Potatodai that I would find a way for him to get back to his own planet. His spaceship went back without him. You always taught us junior witches that when we made a promise we were not to go back on our word.'*

The warts on Rittop's face got bigger with anger as she listened to what Snizzlezallig had to say. *'You knew that he was in trouble and yet you brought him here. You only brought him here for fun. You were thinking about yourself and not your guest. I did not allow you into this den to behave like this!'* she roared.

'Sooorry!' Snizzlezallig mumbled.

'You should have told us the situation the minute you brought him here,' Rittop scolded. *'You and Gizo will clean out the witch's pot every single morning for the foreseeable future.'*

'But, but, that's a terrible job! That horrid sticky pot has zillions of ingredients in it,' wailed Gizo. *'Some of them stick like glue to the side of the pot.'*

'And the smell is vile,' piped in Snizzlezallig. *'Give us an easier punishment, please!'*

Rittop was not in the mood to bargain. *'Take it or leave,'* she growled. *'You got yourself in to this mess.'*

'Okay, okay, I'll take it,' agreed Gizo, who was very conscious that Snizzlezallig was watching her from a distance. *'I will clean it myself. I should not have gotten so involved with our guest. Release him now, please.'*

'Zigglop, zalliuor, birtueeeee,' mumbled Rittop. *'You are freee, said by meee.'*

Potatodai shook himself and stood up. He felt the extra two legs disappear and his body go back to its normal size. He wondered what was going to happen next. This whole Earth adventure was turning in a living nightmare.

Rittop spoke again. *'Kindly get that thing out of here this instant. This is no place for aliens. As for you, Snizzlezallig, you should be ashamed of yourself for bringing him here in the first place.'*

'Okay, spud, let's go!' cackled Snizzlezallig. *'Get onto my broomsticky now and holdy onto me very tightly, in case you get dizzy and fall off.'*

As they left, Gizo pulled her big hat down over her eyes, so no one could see that she was crying. She had made such a mess of things. She had fallen out with her friend. She had caused the senior witches to cast nasty spells on Potatodai. Worst of all, she had to clean that rotten pot every day. She decided that very minute, that she would never, ever be jealous of anyone again. She would admire from a distance, but that would be her lot.

Rittop watched in amazement as Snizzlezallig dragged the funny-looking spud onto her broomstick. *'You know that our spells do not work above fifty miles high in the sky; how did you think you are going to get him back to his planet?'* she asked.

'I'm not sure,' confessed Snizzlezallig. *'But I do have one idea. I will have to eat humble pie and ask the e- mails.'*

Rittop was stunned. *'Have you gone mad?'* she roared. *'Have you lost your mind? Those e-mails are our enemies. They keep crashing into us in the sky and now you want to ask for their help. If they take you prisoner, we will not come to rescue you.'*

But Snizzlezallig wasn't going to give up. *'Please, Rittop, please let me try,'* she begged. *'I cannot break my promise to Potatodai.'*

The rest of the witches nodded their heads in agreement. *'We neeever break a promise,'* they crooned together. *'Snizzlezallig is a veeery good and trusted trainee witch. Let her help him find a way.'*

'Maybe her little chat with the e-mails will help us to get on with them a little better in the future,' advised Zag, an intelligent and trusted witch. *'Sometimes making up is better than fighting.'*

Potatodai jumped for joy when he saw them coming around to the idea. He knew nothing about these e-mail things, but he would try anything to get home. Nothing could be worse than this. He never, ever wanted to be a rat or a football again. It was horrible. Imagine lifting his leg to go to the toilet! If Princess Zamba ever saw him doing that she would be horrified.

Snizzlezallig trembled with fear as the broomstick took off. *'Are you really scared of the e-mails?'* he asked.

'I don't want to say,' sniffed Snizzlezallig. *'We witches are notty meant to be afraid of anything.'*

Potatodai begged her to tell him all about them. *'I want to know who they are and what they do,'* he pleaded. *'I need to tell my Princess all about them.'*

'You have a habit of getting around me, spuddy. Okay, we will take a spinny through the sky, as it will take me a few minutes to tell you the story. Maybe it is best you know about them before we meet them in person.'

Over and back, back and over, they whizzed through the sky as Snizzlezallig did her best to explain the e-mails to Potatodai. *'Have you ever seen a compuuuter, spuddy?'* she asked. Potatodai shook his head. *'I guessed that,'* she giggled. *'Well, I must admit, witches do not know much about them either. On some dark winter nights, we sneak down to Earth, pick a house where the curtains are open, and we sit at the windowsill to watch and listen.*

'Compuuuters help the earthlings. I don't know how they existed before computers were born. Anyway, that is a story for another day. We thought we didn't know a lot about things, but you fruity-veggie-aliens don't seemy to have a clue at all.'

Potatodai was getting a little impatient. *'Tell me about the crazy e-mail messenger people,'* he begged. *'Why are they whizzing up and down the sky, and what have they got to do with computers down on Earth? I am all confused. Please hurry up; I do need to get going back to Zibazilia. Princess Zamba will be worried sick about me. She will think I have died.'*

'Cool it, spud! I will tell youuuuuu,' Snizzlezallig said as she adjusted her bum on the broomstick. *'Are you comfy, spud?'* she asked, continuing with her story before her passenger had time to answer. *'Earthlings send messages to each other all the time and these messages, which the compuuuter sends, are called e-mails. Earthlings think they are smarty but they are not. They can be sooo selfish; they never stop to ask themselves how their messages travel from one computer to another in the space of seconds.'*

'And how do they?' asked Potatodai.

Snizzlezallig was getting tired of the constant interruptions. *'Shut your gobby, spuddy, and let me finish. Some of these computers are located thousands and thousands of miles from each other. Earthlings just take e-mails for granted. They don't appreciate what a wonderful job they are doing, carrying their silly billy messages all over the world and in such a short time.'*

Potatodai was fascinated. Planet Earth, ugly witches, e-mails, it was all too much to take in.

Snizzlezallig adjusted her bum on the stick one more time. *'I am always saying those e-mails should go on strike; then earthlings would realise how useful they are. As for us witches, they drive us crazy taking up all our space in the sky. So in one way you could say I feely sorry for the e-mails and in the other way I hate them.'*

'But why are you witches so frightened of them? They look quite cute to me. Look! There goes one. He has a big heart in his hand.'

Snizzlezallig ventured a small smile. *'I must admit, I likey him. His name is Amouras and he is the Love Mail. He carries all types of love messages around the world.'*

Potatodai was stunned. Was this the Amouras that was brought to see his Princess?

Snizzlezallig scratched a large pimple on her wrinkly neck and thought for a moment. *'You see, twenty years ago nobody had heard of an e-mail and witches could fly around to our hearts' content. All we had to worry about were planes, and even they can only travel at a certain height.*

'Now we have very little space in the sky. The emails are zooming uppy and down, down and uppy, all day and night. They never seem to take a rest. If we dare cross paths with an e-mail we are in biiig trouble. They blame us for slowing them down; they blame us for everything! They say that they are bringing very important messages to other earthlings, and that witches are nothing but a waste of space.

'Anyway, live and let live, that's what I say. I wish we could all be friends, and that they would realise that we are important too. Imagine, they think they are superior to us! Witches have been in the sky for thousands of years.'

Snizzlezallig glanced at her broomstick mirror. She could see that her passenger still had a very puzzled look on his cute spud face. His little daisy eyes were fluttering in the wind. She made up her mind at that moment that he was the most beautiful creature she had ever met in her whole life. She wished she could own him and stare at him forever and ever. But, even in a witch's world, life just did not work like that.

'Do you understand sooo far what I am saying, spud?'

Potatodai jumped to attention. *'Go on,'* he gulped. *'I have never heard anything so interesting in my whole life. Just wait until I tell my Princess. Of course, that is if I ever see her again. You are such an interesting witch and you have such superior knowledge of the skies.'*

Snizzlezallig's face lit up with pride. She was always called stupid in the witches' den and now, here was someone who was so delighted to hear her talk and who depended on her. It was nice to feel important for once.

Potatodai noticed a big black hair sticking out of the pimple on her neck. *'Yuck,'* he thought.

'Whatcha looking at, spud?' Snizzlezallig asked, secretly hoping that he was not staring at her neck. She knew she had lots of pimples and ugly warts, but her witch doctor told her that they would disappear as she got older. She longed for that day to hurry up.

And as the strange-looking pair whirled around the sky, Snizzlezallig told Potatodai everything she knew about the e-mails.

'See, once an e-mail leaves the earthling's computer, it moves at an extraordinary speed, so fast, in fact, that it is invisible to the earthling's eye. The earthling writes a message and then pressy the send button on their computer. Then the e-mail shoooooots out the back of their computer and makes for the nearest window or door facing northwards. They can bend and stretch, and roll into a tiny ball, so they get through the smallest crack or even under a door.

'If earthlings ever have problems sending an e-mail then it means that the mail just cannot find a crack or a window to get out. The e-mail will then sit patiently in the computer's outbox and wait for someone to open a door or a window. Then it is gone. I have to admit it, it's very impressive.

'Globber, one of our elder witches, has been trying for years to make up a spell which would help us to move at the same speed but she hasn't come up with anything yet.'

'Go on, go on,' Potatodai encouraged Snizzlezallig. He was getting a little impatient. 'What happens then?'

Snizzlezallig roughly pushed her hair out of her beady eyes. 'The e-mails shoot up through the sky in a straight line until finally they reach the entrance to two looong very narrow tunnels called the MTs – the Mail Tunnels.

'The MT tunnel divides into two smaller tunnels known as the HP tunnel and the LI tunnel. HP means High Priority and LI means Low Importance. It all depends on the type of message.'

'The e-mail carriers working in the HP tunnel need to have a college degree because they are in charge of the very, very important mails, like messages to kings and queens and government ministers, and messages from people who really, really want make up after a big row.

'The HP staff are given very severe punishment if they are not up to scratch, and sometimes they are demoted to the LI tunnel.

'To the right of those two tunnels lies the MC tunnel, meaning Mission Complete. All the e-mails go there after they deliver their mails. This one divides into a HP and an LI tunnel too. The e-mails wait here until an earthling is about to send a mail and then they then dash down to their computers.'

Potatodai was spellbound. 'Wait until my Princess hears all this! Maybe it was worth missing the Ziggercraft after all.'

'The boss in charge of the e-mails is called Liame. He gave himself that name because Liame is e-mail spelt backwards. Isn't that clever!'

'Really clever,' agreed Potatodai.

'Liame is a bit of a toughie, but I must admit he does a very good job. Each e-mail must report to him as he either goes out of the tunnel or comes back in. This is how Liame keep tracks of the hours they work and how long it takes them to get from one computer to the next.'

'Sounds like hard work,' said Potatodai.

'The lazy ones get fired. There are more than one hundred and eighty e-mails in all. To get the job they must be fast movers with loads and loads of energy. They must also have a very good sense of direction and must get on well with their workmates. If they crash into one another in the sky, they just get on with things and don't lay blame on each other.

'They are named according to what they carry. The Birthday Mail carries all the birthday messages. Groupie carries all the fan-club e-mail messages. Amouras is the love mail and he carries messages of love from one person to another. He is one of the busiest and the best-paid. Love is so important, isn't it?' cooed Snizzlezallig, as she cast a sly look at her broomstick mirror.

Potatodai hoped that he was not expected to give an answer. *'What a wonderful job, an e-mail messenger,'* said Potatodai, hoping to get the conversation back on track.

By the time the long-winded explanation of the e-mails had ended, Snizzlezallig had spun around the sky seventeen and a quarter times and as her explanation came to an end, she decided to fly over the opening to the two e-mail upward tunnels.

'There they are, just as I told you. The e-mails also sleep in their tunnels, you know…'

Potatodai had heard enough about e-mails to last him a lifetime. It was now time for some action. *'Please Snizzle witch, please find a way for me to get back to my planet at the tip-top of the sky,'* he begged. *'My Princess will be out of her mind with worry about me. The Ziggercraft will have arrived back and nobody will have any answers as to where I am. I know you witches have no spells after fifty miles in the air, but please, I beg of you, do something.'*

'Cool your tongue, spuddy. I have it almost worked out. We're going to get an e-mail to take us to Zibazilia.'

'Us!' echoed Potatodai, in a fearful tone. *'What do you mean "us"? My Princess would not be expecting a witch to visit. It will be disappointing enough that I have not brought an earthling with me.'*

'Come on, spuddy, chilly outy. I want to be part of the action. If you are going to hitch a ride on an e-maily then I'm coming with you. I will have to ask Liame. This could be difficult – he hates witchies.'

Liame was in a bad mood. He had been having a snooze and did not welcome the fact that somebody woke him. He was in an even worse mood when he saw that it was an ugly, smelly, greasy witch who was waiting to speak with him.

'What do you want, witch?' he asked angrily. 'Oh my, my, what a pong! All I ever hear about you lot are complaints. My e-mails are always bumping into witches in the sky. Why do you not open your beady eyes and keep out of our way. We have a job to do and we have to do it in a big hurry.'

'Don't be so cruel, Liame,' sniffed Snizzlezallig.

'Somebody should banish you lot from the skies. You should take a leaf from the cherubs' book and present yourself as beautifully and as gracefully as they do. Do witches not have grooming or space etiquette classes? Mind you, I would not like the thought of having to groom you crowd.'

Snizzlezallig decided that the only way to get around this angry man was to ignore his nasty comments and to beg and grovel.

'Insult me all you likey, Liame but the help I need is not for me. It is for my spud friend here from Planet Zibazilia.'

'Did you say Zibazilia?' Liame exclaimed. 'That's where my precious Amouras was taken last week! And what is that thing?' He had finally noticed Potatodai.

Snizzlezallig was quickly on the defence. *'No, Mr Liame, sir, this is Spudatodai – I mean, Potatodai. He came to visit Earth but his spaceship went back to Zibazilia without him.'*

Potatodai sat up straight on the back of the broomstick. *'It's true, sir. The Paparasky took your e-mail to see my Princess but he was treated ever so royally, sir. My Princess adored him, and he was ever so helpful. He gave us the strength to pursue our dream and visit the home of our ancestors. Sadly, our Ziggercraft ran short of zonk and went back to Zibazilia without me and now I am stranded.'*

Snizzlezallig spoke again. *'I made a promise to my friend here and I don't want to break it. Can we – I mean, can he – please hitch a ride on one of your e-mails?'*

Liame was disgusted. *'We are professionals doing very important work. It is not our duty to carry passengers, especially aliens that we know nothing about. You have a cheek to even consider asking a question like that.*

'Are you aware that if we do not do a good job, the earthlings have the power to delete my precious e-mails? Do you know how hard it is to get reliable staff these days?'

'Do some grovelling yourself,' Snizzlezallig whispered to Potatodai. *'Put on a saaad spud face or something. Convince him that you have to go home urgently.'*

'Please, Mr Liame, sir,' pleaded Potatodai in a sorrowful voice. *'Zibazilia and my Princess need me. I would not ask you this favour but I am desperate. If you help me, I promise that I will come down to see you again. I will also ask my Princess for a present just for you.'*

'I couldn't care less if I never saw you again, spud!' roared Liame. *'You are of no help to me or my staff.'*

'I may even get you a special invitation to my Planet Zibazilia and only one in a million gets that,' continued Potatodai in desperation. *'Planet Zibazilia allows very few visitors inside its gates. Everybody else is left outside. I bet you didn't know that?'*

Liame thought for a moment and he began to weaken. *'Well, that's different. I like getting invited to special places. And you say you have a Princess? Why yes, of course you have, Amouras told me all about her. I could put an article about my visit to an unknown planet in the E-Mail Newsletter. That would make me very popular. You say you could get me a special VIP invite?'*

'Most definitely, sir,' blubbered Potatodai.

Liame rubbed his head for a moment in deep thought. *'I think a few of my e-mails are going your way very soon. Leave it with me. I'll have to pay them extra wages, of course, but what the heck. There is another condition.'*

'Anything, sir,' Potatodai cried.

Liame glanced over at Snizzlezallig, who was now cowering behind the brushiest part of her broomstick.

'That smelly witch is not allowed to travel on any of my e-mails.'

Potatodai hoped with all his heart that Liame would help him to get home. It would work even better if he did not allow the witch to travel. Potatodai already had enough explaining to do.

'*Stop gossiping and arguing this instant,*' Liame shouted to a few of his e-mails who were huddled together at the entrance to the HP tunnel.

'*What's happening, sir?*' Potatodai asked innocently. '*Why are they fighting?*'

Liame clenched his rather out-of-shape antennae together. '*It's called spam, spud. Horrible earthlings should not send this kind of useless rubbish. I told my e-mails that if they get given this trash to send, they must dump the message halfway up the sky before it gets to another computer. Messages like that do not deserve to be sent.*

'*Just now one of those mails got deleted by a human because she carried spam in to his computer, so she is very cross. She is now barred from her job and I will have to replace her.*'

'*And what happens when a mail gets deleted?*' Potatodai asked. 'What happens to them then?'

'*A very intelligent question, that is,*' answered Liame. '*Deleted mails are named and shamed. Their career is over, so they just hang about the skies and cause trouble wherever they go because they are so bored.*'

'*How do the e-mails have enough energy to fly all day long and at such great speed?*'

Liame appeared quite chuffed with Potatodai's interest. '*Oh, spud, that is easy,*' he said. '*We pump them with a special mail gas that lets them travel even faster than light. They go to the top of the sky, and once they bounce off the top of the sky, their antennae come into operation. The antennae then lead them downwards to their destination.*

'Now, if you have no further questions, I must depart. Wait here please and an e-mail will come presently to take you to your destination. Do not even attempt to offer him any bribes; the wages he gets from me are sufficient. And remember, that ugly witch is not allowed to travel. I would not have her within a mile of my e-mails. Message understood?'

'Thank you, Mr Liame, sir, thank you with all my heart,' beamed Potatodai. *'I will not forget my promise to take you to Planet Zibazilia. I will be in touch.'*

'Don't think you can make a habit of these journeys, spud!' Liame roared as he left.

'Did you hear that, Snizzlezallig?' Potatodai said with delight. *'Liame is arranging for me to go home.'*

Snizzlezallig was anything but happy. Her face began to scrunch up as if she was going to cry. *'I feel as if I have let you down, you cute spud. I would looove to be able to take you back to your planet.'*

Potatodai's little potato lips formed in to a big smile. *'Think nothing of it, and remember, Snizzlezallig, without you I would never have got to spend time on Planet Earth. I owe you big time. The next time I am down, we must meet up for a long chitty-chat.'*

At that very moment, an extremely colourful looking e- mail wearing all kinds of flags came thundering out of the HP tunnel. Liame waved him down and had a quick word in his ear.

'Okay, boss,' he replied. *'I get the picture. Is that the alien over there?'* Liame nodded.

'Hop on, alien!' he yelled to Potatodai. *'Quickly, quickly! I can't stop; I am just building up speed.'* Potatodai jumped on, and the email continued: *'I hear you are going to Zibazilia. Is that the funny planet covered in rocks with the huge palace in the middle?'*

'That's it, that's the one!' squeaked Potatodai, thrilled that someone knew his little home planet.

'Hey, come to think of it, I'm sure I bounced up there one night and I saw you dangling your legs off the edge of the planet. I remember I felt a bit sorry for you then and now, here you are! Wonders will never cease. It's a small universe, isn't it?'

Potatodai tried to respond but he could not get a word in edgeways.

'By the way, I'm called Politicio. I carry the e-mails for all the politicians in the world. I'll admit I don't understand a word of political lingo, but I am really privileged to have this important job. Liame said I am good at keeping secrets so that's why he chose me to carry these messages.'

Potatodai began to relax; he felt he was in good company and his heart began to beat a little slower.

'I suppose I can take my time today because I have been given a very easy job. I just have to let the politicians know that they will be getting a bigger clothing allowance. Of course, if my message had anything to do with running the country I would not be dilly-dallying.'

The speed at which Politico flew was incredible. Potatodai had turned around to say goodbye to Snizzlezallig, but she was already was nothing but a tiny dot in the sky.

She may not have been too easy on the eye but she had helped him to get back to Zibazilia. He felt a little sorry that he did not have some sort of thank-you gift. He could still smell the awful smell of potion on his face and hands. The witch looked and smelt awful, but Princess Zamba often told him that personality was much more important than looks, and he would never forget her great kindness in bringing him to and from Planet Earth.

a very cross deleted e-mail

He had a funny feeling that he had not seen the last of Snizzlezallig, but he did know one thing for sure: he would never, ever, ever give her the kissy wissy thing she was looking for.

'Its Zibazilia!' screamed Potatodai as they made a turn in the sky. 'I'm home, I'm home! I cannot wait to see Princess Zamba and Glitterati and everybody else. I am even happy to see Carrotpeaash and Turnipear.'

His private thoughts, the journey, and the conversation with Politicio had been so exciting that Potatodai had not a clue how long the journey had taken. All he knew was that it was dark on Planet Zibazilia and he would have to attend immediately to his security duties.

'Thank you, thank you, thank you with all my heart, Mr Politico! You have done me such a big favour. If there is ever anything I can do for you, let me know,' he shouted as he jumped off. 'I've already promised your boss a visit here. Oh, and I hope the politicians enjoy their new clothes.'

When he looked around, Politico had vanished into the night sky and he was all alone.

Princess Zamba was fast asleep in her strawberry-scented feather bed when Zope, her favourite little page, ran up and tapped her on the hand.

'Wake up, Your Highness, wake up,' he whispered loudly. *'I have some great news for you.'*

'What … what is it, Zope?' asked Princess Zamba as she sleepily rose from her strawberry-scented pillow. *'What could be so important? I have been awake half the night worrying about Potatodai, and just when I fall asleep you go and wake me up again. I shall have to punish you if it is something which could have waited until morning.'*

'But, but, that's what I want to tell you about,' answered Zope. *'It's Potatodai! He is back! I saw him on sentry duty a moment ago when I went out to get some air.'*

'Oh my gilly golly gish,' whooped the Princess. *'Get me my furry slippers and a coat. I must go out there now.'*

Zope was puzzled. *'Now, Your Highness? But it's the middle of the night.'*

'Oh I know, Zope, but my friend Potatodai is back and I feel ever so pleased. I must go and see him. I want to find out about his journey and how he managed to get back to Zibazilia without a Ziggercraft. I have been out of my mind with worry. Extract some juice from the ears of a junior bananaplum and bring it to me. Potatodai must be very tired and I want him to have some energy.'

Princess Zamba shuddered with the cold as she emerged from her bed and uttered some strict instructions to her little page: *'I do not want you or any of the other pages to tell Carrotpeaash or Turnipear about this until I speak with Potatodai first. Do you understand?'*

'Yes, Your Highness.'

'Those bodyguards know too much, and too much knowledge for anyone is a bad thing.'

Zope was a little surprised by the Princess's orders, but he did not blink. *'I understand, Your Highness,'* he lied. He loved to see his Princess in a good mood. She had such a pretty face when she smiled, and her beautiful strawberry smell got stronger the louder she laughed.

Zope had not ever told a soul but in fact he really fancied the Princess and he dreamed about her each night. Of course, all he could do was dream. He wished that he had been born with royal blood in his veins.

While he waited for the banana plum to arrive with a glass of his juice, Zope found a woolly scarf for the Princess to wear. He could hear her running around her bedroom in delight as she quickly got dressed.

'Yakeska yoom yoom!' squealed the Princess in delight as she brushed her long golden hair. *'The brain of our planet is back. I cannot wait to hear about Planet Earth! That is, if he ever got there.'*

She sang and she danced, and she almost tripped over her long hair, causing such a racket that two little pages immediately ran to her assistance. A strong strawberry scent filled the entire corridor, so they knew that their Princess was really, really happy, and if she was happy, then they were happy too. A very dark, gloomy bedtime had turned into a bright and exciting awakening.

Less than half an hour later, and with the help of Zope as lookout, Princess Zamba snuck out of the palace through an unused dark staircase. She adored her two bodyguards, Carrotpeaash and Turnipear, but tonight she needed to spend some time alone with Potatodai.

Zope weaved his way in and out between tall, jagged rocks, with the Princess following close behind.

'It's not the normal route, Your Royal Highness,' he explained in an apologetic tone. *'I just want to confuse anyone who may be spying on us or following us. Do you understand, Your Highness?'* The Princess nodded happily.

Finally, they saw Potatodai's shadow in the distance. He was looking quite forlorn, as if he had a thousand and one things on his mind. He was in such deep thought that he didn't hear the Princess and Zope walk up behind him.

'My dear Potatodai,' Princess Zamba whispered. *'I would hug you, but that is something a Princess does not do. How good it is to see you back.'*

Potatodai smiled humbly. *'It is good to be back,'* he answered. *'I have had such an adventure. I cannot quite decide whether it was good or bad, but one way or the other I have brought back loads of information for you. Unfortunately, I have not brought an earthling with me, and I do not think we ever will.*

'I'm so sorry, dear Princess. They are much bigger than I imagined and there is no possible way they would fit into the craft. It would not be balanced properly with their weight.

'Shall I tell you everything now or would you like to wait for another time. Look, I have brought a woolly hat from Earth with me. A little earthling called Jason gave it to me.'

'Tell me everything now,' squealed the Princess with excitement. *'Do not leave out one single detail.'*

'Put your hood up to protect you from the cold, Your Highness,' advised Zope. *'May I also suggest that you wrap the earthling's woolly hat around you? I know you are dying to hear everything now, but it is a very cold night. I will depart now and leave you to talk with your friend.'*

Princess Zamba smiled. *'Thank you, Zope, your help in this matter will be remembered and rewarded.'*

And so, Potatodai began to tell Princess Zamba of Zibazilia about his journey. She gazed in wonder at him when he told her about his meeting with a young earthling and she gasped in further amazement when he told her about the e-mails, the witches, and all the strange things in the sky.

'And you got a ride home on one of these e- mails, is that correct?' the Princess asked on a number of occasions. *'You could say really that they saved your life. I think I will now accept the fact that we are small and that we may never get to meet an earthling.*

'The most important thing is that you are back safe and well, Potatodai. Later, I will sit down with Carrotpeaash, Turnipear, Aspalemon, and some more engineers. We will discuss if it is possible to carry more zonk in our Ziggercraft or maybe build a more powerful, larger machine.'

'I look forward to that,' answered Potatodai happily.

The little Princess smiled sweetly. *'If that is possible, then we may be able to visit Planet Earth again, maybe next year, or the year after. But now, dear Potatodai, it is time for me to go. Please drink all your juice and I will send down a parcel of goodies to you when I get back. I will come and visit you again soon and you can tell me the story in more detail. Tonight, I will sleep. A very big weight has just been lifted from my mind.'*

Potatodai fell into bed in a state of extreme exhaustion the following morning. He quickly went to sleep but had a dream that made him wake in a terrible panic. He was sitting on top of an e-mail and the e-mail got dizzy and kept spinning around. Potatodai was hanging on for dear life, and the dizziness in the dream got so bad that he actually fell out of his hammock.

He then dreamt that he was taking a lift from a deleted mail when the mail exploded halfway up in the sky, and they were both blown to pieces.

He was glad when it was time to get up.

While Potatodai was dreaming, Snizzlezallig the witch was on her broomstick, tearing around the sky like a mad thing.

'I thinky I'm in love, Gizo!' she shouted across to her friend, who was travelling beside her. *'I feel like butterflies are jumping around in my tummy.'*

'In love!' mocked Gizo. *'We witches do not fall in love. We only fall in love with our potions.'*

'I know, Gizo, I know,' sighed Snizzlezallig, *'but this is the strangest feeling I have ever had in my whole life.'*

'Who are you in love with, dare I ask?' taunted Gizo again. *' Did you meet a good-looking earthling on Halloween night?'* Gizo knew that her friend was very secretive, so she did not expect a straight answer.

However, this time she was wrong. Her friend was willing to confide in her even though she had been so mean to her.

'I'm in love with Potatodai.'

Gizo laughed and laughed, and only stopped when the tears fell from her eyes and she got a pain in her tummy. *'Are you sure you haven't put a magic spell on yourself?'* she croaked.

But Snizzlezallig was not impressed. *'I knew I did the wrong thing confiding in you. I don't care what you or aaany of the other witches think. I am determined to see him again and then the laugh will be on the other sidey of your face.'*

'And how do you plan to do that?' sneered Gizo. 'You know our magic spells don't work any higher up than we are now. And you a junior – you only get simple spells now and again.'

'Oh, you witch of little faith,' muttered Snizzlezallig in a faint voice. 'If you were a good friend to me you would trust me and even try to help me.'

'Wait until I tell the other witches tonight,' laughed Gizo. 'Snizzle is in love. Oh my goodness, that is the funniest thing I have heard for many years,' she cackled as she sped home through the sky with the news.

'Gooo on, laugh! But let me tell you one thing, the last laugh is always the best laugh,' Snizzlezallig screamed after her.

'Snizzle is in love with a potato,' sang Gizo as she zigzagged at speed over and back through the blue sky. Her stick almost bent In half as she exploded with big gasps of laughter and she nearly lost her balance on more than a few occasions.

'She's just jealous,' thought Snizzlezallig. 'I saw the way she looked at Potatodai when I brought him to our den. She fancies him too, but she will not admit it. She is a sneaky friend and a sneaky friend is not a good friend. They are only out for themselves.'

That night, Snizzlezallig slunk back to her den. After checking to make sure all the witches were out, she packed her few belongings together in a bag and tied it to the end of her broomstIck.

But Gizo had been watching from a distance and shot through the sky when she spotted her leaving. 'Where do you think you are going? Call yourself a witch,' she hissed. 'You are a scaredy-cat witch. Wait until the senior witches hear that you have gone to run after an alien spud.'

Snizzlezallig ignored her and quickly made her way towards the e-mail tunnels. She folded up her broomstick, put it in her pocket, sat cross-legged on top of a tunnel, and waited. E-mails came out at such great speed that they were gone before she had time to put up her hand to stop them. She decided to stand between the HP tunnel and the LI tunnel; between the two of them, she was convinced someone would stop.

However, seconds later she heard a very loud collision. She had blocked the view of the mails going in to the HP tunnel and, as a result, one of them had banged into a mail carrier from the LI tunnel.

'Now look what you've done!' one mail roared at the other. *'My message has dropped off and I have nothing to carry. I will be sacked!'*

'The messages you carry are not as important as mine,' the other mail shouted back at him. *'Common mails like you should get the sack anyway. You just carry boring e-mails.'*

'Stop it,' Snizzlezallig called out. *'This is all my fault. I was standing in the waaay and blocked the view. Please do not argue. I get enough of that at home.'*

The e-mails were shocked to see the weird-looking creature with the dark cloak and the big, spotty nose looking at them. *'You look like a witch!'* said the younger, more innocent LI mail.

'I am a witch,' agreed Snizzlezallig. *'I need to go to Planet Zibazilia to see a good friend of mine called Potatodai. He came down a few days ago but he had to go back in a hurry. I am now trying to see my dear friend again. Can you give me a lifty please?'*

'We are not allowed to give anyone a lift unless we have permission from Liame. He is away today, so there is no one for us to ask.' The e-mail who spoke looked like a large burger with a white hat. He introduced himself as the Foody Mail. *'I deliver e-mails about fancy*

food,' he boasted. *'Earthlings love nice food and fancy restaurants. Do you think I am going to lower myself to carrying a witch with me? No, no way,'* and with that little speech he disappeared into the sky, shouting all the way. *'My clients wouldn't want a smelly witch sitting on top of their message. Why don't you go and have a nice hot bath for yourself.'*

Snizzlezallig decided to ignore him. The other mail had also disappeared into the sky without giving her much thought. She hoped that a nice e-mail would come along.

However, an hour and a half went by and Snizzlezallig had started to become worried. Dozens and dozens of e-mails were speeding past her. Most of them just stared or giggled at her. Two hours passed, and she wondered if she should go back to her den.

'Maybe it would be better to waity until tomorrow and speak to Mr Liame again,' she thought.

She would remind him of Potatodai's invite to Zibazilia. Maybe he could bring her there himself.

'I'm just so happy that they bought a Beamer instead of a Mercedes,' boomed a voice above her head suddenly. *'Hi witch,'* he chirped *'I'm the New and Second-Hand Car Mail and my name is Porcha. So many earthlings have nice cars sitting outside their houses and its all thanks to my messages. I have such a great job. Anyway, why are you hanging around here? Speak loudly please. I can't slow down so I will have to keep whizzing around your head.'*

Snizzlezallig told her tale of woe, and being the happy-go-lucky e-mail that he was, Porcha decided to give her a lift to Zibazilia.

'Can I confide in you?' Snizzlezallig asked as they sped through the sky.

'Sure,' smiled Porcha.

'Witchies don't usually get on with e-mails, but I have to say I really admire you. I thought we witchies were the fastest thing in the whole sky but now I know we are only second best.'

Porcha blushed. 'Gee, thanks,' he beamed. 'I never got a compliment like that before.'

Snizzlezallig began to look a little worried. 'What will happen if Mr Liame finds out that you gave me a lift? Will he sack you?'

'What he won't find out won't trouble him,' grinned Porcha. 'It's all in the name of friendship and goodwill. Just keep your head well down and take off that silly hat. I do not want other e-mails to notice that I have a passenger.'

'But, but, witches are never seen without their hats,' Snizzlezallig explained. 'We must at all times keep our brains warm because our spells are hidden amongst our brain cells.'

'Okay, okay,' said Porcha, 'but please do your best to keep your head down. I do not want you to draw attention to us.'

Shortly after the journey started, there was trouble. *'How could I have such baaad luck,'* thought Snizzlezallig. She had spotted someone she really did not want to see. Her head was bent so low that it almost touched her knees.

That person was Santa Claus. He and his reindeers were making their way northwards across the sky. They were quite some way in the distance, but Santa never missed a trick. His space telescope never let him down. He shouted over at Porcha.

'Don't tell me that it is you e-mail lot again,' he yelled. *'I am going to sue you! Two weeks ago, Rudolph was going on an errand for me and one of you e-mails crashed in to him. He sprained his ankle! What would have happened if this was Christmas time? Well?'*

Porcha did not answer so Santa continued: *'A few years ago there was no such thing as an e-mail and we had a bit of peace and quiet in the sky. Now its nothing but commotion from dawn to dusk, and from dusk till dawn.'*

Santa was so angry that his face turned a bright shade of red when he spotted Snizzlezallig. *'Don't tell me that you are friendly with these e mails!'* he growled.

'We are … I mean, we are not … I mean we might beee,' mumbled Snizzlezallig.

Santa moved closer for a better look. *'I though you witches kept to yourselves. I do not know one of you is worse. Last year, I brought a big box of Lego to a little child in Ireland and you witches turned it into a spider with fifteen legs. Is that true?'*

'It's true, Santa,' admitted Snizzlezallig, *'and I'm veeery sorry. I am the culprit. My senior witch gave me a Christmas present of a big spell and I wanted to try it out. All I wanted was a bit of fun on Christmas morning, but I did not realise the misery it would cause the little child. I tried to turn the spider back into Lego, but it would not work. I had only been given one spell.'*

'Well, don't let it happen this year,' warned Santa. *'As for you e- mails, just keep out of our way please. From now until Christmas we will be very busy.'*

Santa was not leaving without getting a little bit of news. He decided to give Snizzlezallig a good questioning. *'What are you doing travelling on an e-mail anyway. Haven't you got enough to keep you busy making magic potions?'*

'None of yooour business,' answered Snizzlezallig cheekily. She hated people who asked her loads of questions. *'Oh, by the way, what did you have for your breakfast? It must have been loads as you have suuuch a big tummy.'*

'You naughty witch,' laughed Santa, who was now beginning to take the whole thing in good spirit. *'Must go now. Be good, you lot, won't you? Do remember one thing. Christmas is coming, and it is the season of goodwill. Do not forget to respect everyone you meet in the sky.'*

'Are you married, witch?' Porcha later asked, quite unexpectedly. Snizzlezallig hesitated, then said nothing.

'Well are you, or are you not?'

Snizzlezallig spluttered a little and then cleared her throat. *'Well, you see witches just happen. A baby witchy appears out of nowhere; it's all done by magic.'*

'What are you on about?'

'There are no boy witches, so we don't have anyone to fall in love with. Well that was the way until I met Potatodai,' said Snizzlezallig. Porcha frowned.

'But I still like you,' Snizzlezallig cooed. It would be so awful to hurt this kind e-mail's feelings.

At that moment, the very top of the sky came into view. Snizzlezallig got very, very excited. *'Looky over there!'* she shrieked. *'That must be Zibazilia. I can smell the fruit. It's delicious! It's exactly as Potatodai described it, a yummy smell and loads of rocks, and yes, there is a palace with a moat around it right in the middle.'*

'Well I don't know anything about it, and I don't intend to learn,' answered Porcha. *'I wouldn't want to be kidnapped. My friend Amouras had a lucky escape last week. You are a very brave witch to consider going there.*

'So it is here I bounce off the top of the sky and continue my journey downwards. You will have to jump, witch.'

'I'm not jumping anywhere,' growled Snizzlezallig. *'If you were a gentleman, you would drop me at the gate. Please?'* she begged.

'Okay, okay,' agreed Porcha, quite intrigued by this cheeky creature. *'But be warned, if I get kidnapped then you will have to get your friend Potatodai to free me.'*

On looking more closely at the situation, Porcha discovered that the roof of the palace almost touched the sky and the sides were covered in a strange material. There was only one large entrance gate, and from it hung a huge padlock. The whole palace looked as if it was surrounded by a moat filled with a gluey substance.

'Now, what do you want me to do?' Porcha asked.

'I think I will get off close to the tallest rock and hang around for a while to get to know the surroundings. I know Potatodai will have come out to do his sentry duty. I will try to find him.'

'Jump now!' yelled Porcha. *'This is the highest rock and I am taking such a chance. I could be shot down or anything by these aliens. Nice meeting you!'*

'Nice meeting you tooo,' said Snizzlezallig as she 'shook hands' with her messenger's unusual-shaped antennae.

Porcha was ever so pleased to escape. He had never seen anything like this witch in his whole life and he was not sure if he ever wanted to see anything like her again either. Deep down there was something he liked about her, but he could not put his antennae on it.

But Porcha had not got away as lightly as he thought.

'Would it be possible for you to call for me on your way back up here again?' asked Snizzlezallig, in the nicest voice she could manage. *'I may need a fast getawaaay.'*

Porcha laughed. *'You must be joking, witch. I may have to hang around the car dealers' computers for a while; they may want to send back answers with me. Even if I wanted to pick you up, I wouldn't be able to say when it would be.'*

'I'm so scared,' Snizzlezallig begged. *'What if Potatodai never got back here? I might be all on my own!'* But Porcha was already almost out of sight.

Snizzlezallig examined her surroundings. Several tall, thin rocks loomed here and there in the distance, so it was easy to creep from one to the other without getting noticed.

Potatodai had definitely said that he did sentry duty at night, so she hoped that she would spy him somewhere. She decided to have a good snoop around first.

From time to time, a wave of fear overcame her. She might be stranded on Planet Zibazilia forever and nobody would be able to rescue her. Potatodai may not want her and the whole planet may banish her just as they banished Potatodai.

'Stop thinking stupid things,' she warned herself, but her mind continued to work overtime. She even had witchbumps on her arms with the fear of it all. Her nose was cold and there was sweat on her forehead.

She wondered if people do crazy things when they are in love. Then again, she was a witch, and witches did not fall in love. At least that's what her friend Gizo said.

'Oh, deary me,' she thought. 'I'm so confused. If I don't love Potatodai then why have I still got butterflies in my tummy wummy?'

There was not a sound on the Planet of Zibazilia as Snizzlezallig slowly walked about. The ground was very rough and she had to tread very carefully.

She gasped as suddenly she came face to face with the front of the most magical palace she had ever seen in her entire life. *'Not even a magic spell could make anywhere this nice,'* she thought. *'It looks even better than it did from a distance. I thought Potatodai was exaggerating when he told me but he waaasn't.'*

For a moment, she shivered and felt rooted to the spot.

The palace of Zibazilia, home to all 155 Zibazilians, was indeed spectacular. The bottom was made of rock, the second level looked as if it was covered in very colourful tiles, and the top two sections were made out of a mixture of gold and silver diamonds. Even at night it glittered very brightly.

There were windows everywhere, and each was adorned with red triangular and blue circular lights. Steps led down to an underground section, probably used by servants and Zibazilians of lesser importance. The palace itself was surrounded by a very deep moat full of a very sticky-looking gluey substance.

'I wouldn't like to fall into that,' thought Snizzlezallig. *'I would be in a reeeally sticky situation then, wouldn't I?'*

Insects flew here, there and everywhere, probably drawn by the delicious fruity smell. The locks on the palace gates were so large that they glittered even at a great distance.

Snizzlezallig pinched herself to make sure that she wasn't dreaming. But she was not! Everything was real. She was on Planet Zibazilia standing in front of the most magnificent yet teeny-weeny palace she had ever seen in her whole life. She wished all the other witches could see this. They would never believe her.

Now and again, she thought she could hear the sound of very low voices. She thought it might be the humming of the insects, but as she got closer, she could hear them more clearly. The voices stopped, started, and then stopped again.

Snizzlezallig carefully made her way to the right-hand side of the palace. The noise appeared to come from behind a large rock. Slowly, quietly she crept forward. She could vaguely see shadows.

'Ouchy wouchy!' she screamed to herself as she trod on an insect. Its hard shell crunched under her foot. She wondered if space bugs could talk. Oh dear, she was getting more confused by the minute. She dearly wished that Porcha would come back and take her home, or that Potatodai would come along and rescue her.

There she was a few weeks ago, flying about the sky like an ordinary junior witch, minding her own business. How could she possibly have landed herself in such a terrible mess? Things like this did not just happen to witches.

Slowly and with great care, she edged her way closer to where she thought she heard the voices. *'Over … Throw,'* said a voice quite clearly from behind a rock close to where she stood. She smiled a relieved smile when she realised that she had stumbled across a space game.

It was nice to see that the Zibazilians were having a bit of fun, even if it was the middle of the night. Maybe the younger ones only came out by night.

The game sounded like a kind of hide-and-seek. Yet she could see no one and nobody moved, so how could it possibly be a game?

Sensing danger, Snizzlezallig decided not to go any closer. The air was also very humid and she suddenly felt very sleepy. *'No, no, no!' she thought, 'I must not fall asleep now. I must find my friend first.'*

The whispering got rapidly louder and more excited, and the scared witch realised that this was anything but a game. The terrible truth dawned on Snizzlezallig. *'Over … Throw … Overthrow!'* Somebody was planning a takeover!

'*Trusty me,*' Snizzlezallig thought. *'I'm only seven minutes and six seconds on a new planet and I find myself mixed up in something sinister.'*

The conversation continued for some time. One very deep voice stood out above the rest. *'I want to build my headquarters on Zibazilia because it is central to everywhere.'*

'*And when did you get this notion into your head?*' asked another voice.

Snizzlezallig's heart began to pound so fast that she hoped that no one would hear it. She tried to take deep breaths, but it didn't seem to make much difference.

'*Once that Princess is gone, I will be able to take complete control of the planet,*' said big voice. '*But remember, I will not forget those who helped me. They will have a position of great authority on Planet Zibazilia and will be respected by all.*'

'*But didn't you try something like this a few years ago?*' asked voice number two in an exaggerated whisper.

'*Yep, that's right,*' agreed big voice. '*I tried to destroy them but that stupid Hapigleamatos foiled the plot. I have never forgiven him for that. I thought he was my friend but now he is my enemy. When I have taken over Zibazilia, everybody will see me as his or her God. I will then get revenge on my enemies.*'

'*And who are your enemies?*' asked a timid voice number three.

'The person who foiled my plot, and anybody who I find out was connected to him of course. Were you not listening?' answered big voice angrily. *'I hate having to repeat myself. Nobody on Planet Zibazilia has been nice to me. They are such a stuck-up bunch. Just because they look and smell pretty doesn't mean that they can snub everybody.'*

'We like you regardless of who you are or what you are,' echoed a few voices together.

Snizzlezallig wondered if the other voices were all Zibazilians and who 'big voice' could be. She shook with fear from head to toe. She wondered if Potatodai was part of this gang, but none of the voices she heard had sounded like his. Of course, people could change their voices, couldn't they?

All she knew was that a plot was underway to overthrow the beautiful Princess and to take over Planet Zibazilia. It was all ever so scary, and here she was, all alone.

She decided that she must get the news to the Princess as soon as possible. But the conversation behind the rock continued for a little longer and Snizzlezallig became stiff and cold and very sleepy. The voices became lower and lower, as the plot appeared to thicken. It was impossible at this point to hear what everybody was saying.

She so wished that she would meet Potatodai and he would lead her to the Princess. Maybe he had been on duty and overheard the conversation as well? Or maybe he was part of it! *'Mixy uppy,'* she mumbled to herself. *'Yes, it's all very mixy uppy and my spuddy is missing.'*

When she drifted off, Snizzlezallig dreamt about Gizo's homemade bat-wing soup garnished with morning dew.

Snizzlezallig woke to the sound of someone hissing into her ear: 'Who are you and what are you doing on our Planet?'

'How did you get here?' spat another voice.

Snizzlezallig opened her eyes to see two very unusual looking creatures standing beside her. One looked like a squashed carrot and a small pea with anaemia, and the other was a mixture of a turnip and a big green pear.

'We asked you a question,' they both hissed together. *'One of our pages spotted you lying here and asked us to come immediately. We want an answer.'*

Snizzlezallig felt her heart pounding. She felt that it could burst at any time.

'Our Princess does not take kindly to visitors, and unannounced ones at that,' said the thin one.

This must be the two bodyguards that Potatodai had told her about. Yes, Carrotpeaash and Turnipear. Snizzlezallig remembered him telling her that they both had jealous natures, but that they adored the Princess and looked after her so well.

It was now broad daylight and dozens of little fruity veggie leafy Zibazilians walked and played amongst the rocks. They looked so tiny and cute and colourful. There were bananas, grapes, plums, melons, cauliflowers, oak trees and loads more, all mixed up together. It was such an unusual sight.

'Well?' said the carrot pea. 'We asked you a question. Have you lost your tongue? That is, if you had one in the first place.'

Snizzlezallig shook with fear. 'I flew here myselfy. I only wanted an adventure. I'm from a planet called Pog, about ten thousand space miles from here,' she lied, all in one breath. She was determined not to get Potatodai into any trouble.

'And what is your business here?' asked the fat one. He spoke with a squishy type of voice.

'I, I saw your palace glittering and I was just being nosey,' fibbed Snizzlezallig. 'I just haaad to come and see it.'

But the bodyguards were having none of it. 'We know you are lying. Do you think we are fools?' said the pear with the turnip head. 'We heard Potatodai telling our Princess all about you.'

'I don't know what you are talking about,' mumbled Snizzlezallig.

'Potatodai said you had a long nose with warts on it and that you wore a long coat,' said the anaemic squashed carrot. 'Go on, admit it. You are that witchy creature he was talking about, aren't you?'

'I tell you I am telling the truthy,' Snizzlezallig replied. She was determined not to get her friend and the one she loved into trouble.

The two creatures whispered together for a moment. Then one of them pulled a very tight ball of steel wire from his belt.

'We must take you captive and present you to our Princess,' hissed the fatter of the two. 'Between us, we will decide what is to be your fate. If you try to escape without our permission, then you will be very, very sorry. Do you understand?'

Snizzlezallig was petrified. *'Yessy,'* she replied hoarsely. Why, oh why could witches only use spells within a certain witchy radius of their home!

'You will come with us now to the palace. Nobody puts the life of our Princess in danger. You should have reported to us the minute you arrived here.'

'But it was nighty and it was darky,' answered Snizzlezallig in a shaky voice. *'There was nobody abouty.'*

The carrot pea with the ash on his head spoke after a few seconds. *'Shut it and listen. You will have to wait until our Princess is ready to receive us. Make sure you have the truth ready to tell her.'*

The turnip pear whispered something, and the squashed carrot put his hand to his head. It looked as if he had just thought of something.

'It may be several hours before our Princess Zamba is ready to receive you,' he said. *'This is a very special day on our planet. Today, two of our population are getting married and there will be great celebrations. Our Princess is guest of honour. She must not be disturbed and especially not by an ugly smelly thing like you.'*

Both bodyguards laughed nastily.

'Come with us,' they said in unison. *'You will be locked up until Her Royal Highness is ready to receive you.'*

Carrotpeaash punched in a long code, while Turnipear stood behind him making sure that nobody saw the password.

'Turn away,' he growled. *'Turn away, I said – or else!'*

The golden gate over the sticky moat creaked slowly open. Snizzlezallig was escorted through the gate, into the palace, and down a very long corridor. Down, down they went. As they descended, the lower corridors of the palace began to smell of roasting chestnuts and bleach.

'Get on all fours. You are much too large to stand up in here,' said one of the bodyguards.

Snizzlezallig's stomach felt sick. It was bad enough crawling on all fours, but this smell was much, much worse than the worst potion that the senior witches had ever made.

They passed a very large dining room that had a large menu pinned to the door. The squashed carrot stopped to have a look.

'Oh, goodie,' he said to the turnip head. *'The pages and the juniors are having grilled snowdrop garnished with beetle wing for dinner. That means that we will be having snowdrop with beetle breast and eyes. Yum, yum, that's my favourite.'*

And then, as if things were not bad enough, Snizzlezallig's black cape got caught in a doorway and she had to yank it free. She decided not to look back in case she had knocked the tiny door of its hinges. Even crawling on all fours was a big ordeal, as the tallest

Zibazilian was only nine inches in height and she was so much taller. Butterflies twirled around her tummy.

Here, there and everywhere little heads appeared out of doors, straining to have a look. Cauliflowers, Brussel sprouts, buttercups – they were all there. It was like a flower and vegetable garden that had come alive and was having a huge party.

A page scurried toward them. 'Attention please! The Princess is taking a break from the wedding. She will shortly come indoors and meet the prisoner.'

Carrotpeaash and Turnipear quickly stood to attention. *'And has the other matter been dealt with, Zope?'* they asked the anxious little page.

'Yes, sirs, everything has been done as requested. Please proceed to the Princess's quarters at once. We must not keep her waiting.'

With great haste, they moved upward again, and as they did the corridor widened. From time to time Snizzlezallig caught glimpses of rooms where rows and rows of yellow, green, and blue little hammocks were fixed securely to the ceiling. Each had its own number, obviously relating to a certain person. It was one sure way to make sure that no one would steal each other's beds.

'I wish Gizo could see this,' thought Snizzlezallig. *'She is always napping in my bed. She says it's much softer than hers and she's probably right because my bed is made of crow's feathers and hers is made of rat's hair.'*

'Look, it's a dinosaur!' screamed a baby Zibazilian to his friend as they both peered out between the cracks of a door.

'Don't be silly,' said the other one. *'Dinosaurs have four legs and they don't have long ugly noses like that.'*

'Then what is it?' the first boy asked, as he slammed the door closed and turned the key so that they would be safe inside.

'Oh no,' thought Snizzlezallig. *'They don't like me here. What will the Princess think? If she doesn't like me, then all is lost.'*

The party had almost reached the top of the palace when Snizzlezallig was thrown roughly into a small room and the door was locked from outside.

'You will stay here until our Princess is ready to receive you, witch,' growled Turnipear. *'Help yourself to a drink of midge mist if you are thirsty. You'll see a small jar of it on the shelf above you. But when it's gone you will not get anymore, so drink it sparingly. I suggest you twirl it in your mouth to wet it, then spit it back in to the jar again.'*

Snizzlezallig herself was half the size of a child earthling. She barely had room to stand up in her cramped surroundings. She wondered what would have happened if Potatodai had managed to persuade an earthling to come with them. They would have been unable to come through the doors of the palace and would have to remain outdoors.

Through a small diamond-shaped window, she spied the wedding in progress in a courtyard below. It looked as if a cucumbertomato was marrying a bananaturnipweed. There was loads of pomp and ceremony, with pages running everywhere with trays of gooey-looking treats. Loud jingly music was playing. It was indeed a truly joyous occasion.

Looking back around the little room, the frightened witch shuddered. She tried the doors, but neither would budge. Even if she could escape, the chances of getting back to her witches' den were extremely slim. Gizo would have missed her by now, and would have a group of witchy friends hunting through the skies for her.

It was silly of her not to have left a message, but she had done the whole thing on impulse and didn't think about the consequences. *'It must be that feeling of love,'* she thought. She had heard the earthlings say that people in love did very strange things.
Once, she even heard an earthling say that love could make or break you.

It was such a coincidence that Amouras had been the e-mail that had already paid a visit to the Princess. Snizzlezallig hoped that Amouras had given the Princess a very detailed explanation of all the love messages he sent to and from the earthlings' computers. Maybe then the Princess would understand why she had followed Potatodai. Maybe she too would understand the strange things that love did.

After what seemed like ages, a hidden trapdoor creaked opened and two little creatures in page uniforms appeared. *'Come with us, prisoner. Her Royal Highness, Princess Zamba of Zibazilia has retired from the wedding and is now ready to receive you.'*

They left the room with one page walking in front of Snizzlezallig and the other walking behind. Turnipear and Carrotpeaash arrived and followed the procession. Carrotpeaash addressed the little pages: *'Release him now and have him walk with us to meet the Princess.'* The pages bowed and scurried away.

The smallest page tapped a secret password onto a diamond shape on the ground with his shoe and a nearby door opened. *'Potatodai! Potatodai!'* screamed Snizzlezallig. *'I thought I would never see you again!*

Potatodai looked deathly pale. *'What are you doing here, witch?'* he asked quietly.

'Walk behind us, Potatodai, and ask no further questions,' grunted Turnipear. *'You are not allowed to speak to our visitor. Anything you say will be used as evidence against you when we meet the Princess. We are fully convinced that this witch has come here to harm Her Royal Highness.'*

Potatodai was quick to answer. *'You are wrong. I am fully convinced that the witch has come here to see me. Only for her, I would never have reached Planet Earth, and she was very sad to see me leave. Please do not judge someone until you have good proof.'*

'Move along. You are in enough trouble.'

The heavy smell of roasting peanuts wafted through the air as the entourage climbed higher and higher up the sparkling stairs. One flight, then two, then three, and finally they were at the very top of the palace. The smallest page quickly ushered everybody into a room that had sparkling windows and plush, spongy kind of carpet. Small glitzy gems adorned the roof. From time to time, they appeared to move and change colour. It was as if they were watching something. The doors were star-shaped and each point of each star was of a different luminous colour. The word 'Punishment' flickered on a neon sign at the top of the room.

'I've been here before,' Potatodai whispered to Snizzlezallig. Snizzlezallig sighed. *'And what did you do to deserve that punishment?'*

'It was the night I was condemned to be a sentry forever by those two bodyguards. This room has been named the Punishment Room ever since. Now because of you, I am here again. Those two were waiting for a chance to get me again. I should never have trusted them.'

'My dear Potatodai, how wrong can you be?' grunted Turnipear, who had overheard the whole conversation. *'Neither Carrotpeaash nor myself mean you any harm. Everything we do is for our Princess. You must understand that her safety comes first. We find it very strange that yesterday we gave you the night off on the Princess's request and suddenly this ugly, smelly witch appears. We suggest you get your act together,'* jeered Turnipear, as both bodyguards left the room.

'Potatodai,' whispered Snizzlezallig. *'I am cold and I am hungry and I am miserable and I am scared.'*

The chauffeur e-mail

Potatodai, still numb with shock, did not flinch. *'What do you want from me?'* he asked sternly. *'I thought we said our goodbyes down on Earth. You helped me but I did not expect you to follow me. Now we are both in a pickle.'*

The door flew open and the bodyguards ran towards them in a rage. *'So, you did lie to us, witch!'* they roared.

'We have a listening device hidden in the ceiling,' boasted Carrotpeaash. *'It is trained to pick up the quietest whisper. You told us*

that you did not know anybody on Planet Zibazilia, but we knew you were telling big porkie pie lies.'

Snizzlezallig wished that she had met Potatodai earlier to get their stories straight. She had really blown everything both for herself, and for him. She had to think fast.

Just then, the light eyes on the wall shone a dazzling red and a concealed partition began to open slowly in the wall to the right of the room. A little page stood with a notepad in his hand.

'That's Zope,' whispered Potatodai. *'He is Princess Zamba's favourite page.'*

'Come with me please,' Zope called in a loud assertive voice. *'Her Highness the Princess is ready to meet you. Please always address our Princess as Her Majesty. She must be shown great respect. Stare straight ahead at all times, and no looking downwards. Only speak when you are spoken to. Do you understand?'*

'Yes, we understand,' Potatodai and Snizzlezallig answered nervously. They entered a room designed in the shape of a crown. It glittered from top to bottom and smelt of all things beautiful and all things nice.

Four little pages entered the room and between them, they carried a golden chair over their heads. In it sat one of the most beautiful creatures that Snizzlezallig had ever seen in her whole life. Her face was quite similar to an earthling's face and her body looked like a glitzy, juicy red strawberry. Her buttercup eyelashes and her little strawberry-shaped eyes sparkled. Her strawberry body was adorned in a coat of coloured bows and tiny diamanté pieces that glittered as she moved.

Snizzlezallig was mesmerised. *'Look, Potatodai; over there! Is that the one they call "Her Royal Highness"?'*

'Yes,' replied Potatodai. 'That is Her Royal Highness, Princess Zamba of Zibazilia. Isn't she so beautiful? She is dressed in her official robe. She only dresses like that when she has some very serious business to attend to.'

A sharp nudge from behind alerted Potatodai to the fact that he had already broken the rules by speaking.

'Apologies, sincere apologies,' he mumbled to all assembled.

Princess Zamba of Zibazilia had a small, dainty face framed by golden ringlets. Even her ears were much smaller than the other Zibazilians'. Her buttercup eyelashes were so long that they covered half her face like giant fans. Her strawberry-shaped eyes were a multitude of colours – green, blue and brown. The smell of fresh strawberry all around her was intoxicating.

The pages gently placed her chair on the ground and then they lifted her onto a very large throne. It was so big that ten little Princesses could have sat on it. Princess Zamba flicked her hair and then she lifted one of her tiny shoes and the toe of the shoe suddenly changed into a mirror. She admired herself for a few seconds, and it was only then that she noticed her visitors.

'I'm ready to receive my guests now,' she whispered loudly to the page closest to her. The visitor and Potatodai were then beckoned forward.

Princess Zamba peered at Snizzlezallig and spoke in a quiet, dignified tone. *'I have to admit I have never seen anyone who looks quite like you. I presume you are the witch I have heard so much about!'*

'Me neither, Your Highness royaaal. I have never seen anyone so gorgeous and stunning as you,' answered Snizzlezallig in the sweetest voice she could muster up. *'I am blown awaaay with your beauty. We come from different lands, Your Royal Princess, but I hope we can be friends.'*

'Of course we can,' answered Princess Zamba sweetly. *'It isn't often*

I have visitors, but if you are a friend of Potatodai's, then you are a friend of mine. However, I am a little disturbed to find that my bodyguards say that you came here without an invitation. Nobody comes to Planet Zibazilia without an invitation.'

'I understand,' mumbled Snizzlezallig.

The little Princess nodded. *'That is why Potatodai has been locked up and questioned. You must understand that my bodyguards are suspicious of strangers. They are here to protect me. If you can, please explain to me why, and how, you have come to this planet. I am all ears.'*

'Thank you, ma'am – er, I mean Your Highness Royalle,' said Snizzlezallig. *'Thanky you for saying nice things. I do sooo apologise for coming to your planet without an invite, but you see I did not thinky-inky. I just wanted to meet Potatodai again. I mean no harm. I'm only a common witch. I'm nobody special and I don't go around doing bad things. I wishy-ishy I had come here with good news, but I haven't.'*

'What do you mean, Hizzle?' asked Princess Zamba.

'Actually, its Snizzle for short and Snizzlezallig for long,' said the witch, having picked up a little courage. *'I thinky-inky, in a weird sort of way, that I was meant to come to Planet Zibazilia, because I think you might be in some sort of danger.'*

Carrotpeaash and Turnipear immediately darted forward. *'What do you mean, witch? What kind of trouble? We are here to protect our Princess so we need you to tell us everything you know now. We also need to know why we found you asleep in the palace grounds this morning.'*

'Yes, what exactly do you mean Snizzlezallig?' asked Potatodai in amazement. *'I do hope you have not come here to spin any stories*

or lies. *Carrotpeaash and Turnipear are very smart and they will see through you. Do you understand?'*

'Before we start ma'am, have you any soup?' asked Snizzlezallig, completely forgetting her manners. *'Bat or grasshopper soupy will do, if you have it. I'm really cold and tired and hungry.'*

'Soup!' queried Princess Zamba, looking over at the pages. *'Do we have such a thing?'*

The pages looked at each other in bewilderment and whispered something to the Princess.

'We will make you up a hot liquid from the ears of a space hog,' she said. *'It is very sweet and will give you great energy. It also helps to defuzz the brain.'*

Two pages disappeared in an instant, without waiting to hear if their visitor wanted the drink or not. Potatodai was a little cross with Snizzlezallig's cheekiness, but he was relieved to see that the Princess was not bothered. He was also so pleased that she had agreed to allow the witch to defend herself. He wondered what news she had brought.

Carrotpeaash stood up and addressed the Princess. His voice was loud and clear: *'Your Sweet Highness, it is with much regret that we have had to take you away from the wedding ceremony, but this matter needed your immediate attention.'*

The Princess nodded. *'I'm intrigued. And Potatodai, I am also very surprised to find that the witch followed you here. Did you know she was coming here or did you give her an invite which you forgot to tell me about?'*

But Turnipear was determined to say his piece. *'Your Sweet Highness,'* he gloated. *'We found this witch creature asleep at daybreak when we were just finishing our rounds. She was lying behind a rock. We guessed that this was the witch Potatodai referred to when he got back. It does look as if he has invited her up here without asking permission from anyone. That is why we have brought them both to you.'*

'Dear, dear,' sighed the Princess.

'Not true!' roared Potatodai, his voice quivering with temper. *'Please get your facts correct before you accuse me in the wrong.'*

Princess Zamba stood for a moment. *'Stop it, all of you. Come to me, witch. Come, kneel at my feet and tell me your story. My ears are all yours. You may have your drink as soon as it comes into the room. Silence in the room, please. I need to hear what this witch has to say. Only then shall I make a decision.'*

Snizzlezallig shuffled slowly forward. She stood with her shoulders hunched up and her arms folded. She didn't know whether to bow or not. She wrapped her cloak around her as if to protect her from what was to come.

'Your Royal Highness, this has all been a veeery big mistakey. I did not come here for any other reason only that I wanted to meety Potatodai again. You see I gave him a lift to Earth on my broomstick and we became good friends.'

Princess Zamba smiled. *'Go on, witch, continue your story.'*

'Princess, I missed him and wanted to see him again. I finally ended up getting a lift up to Planet Zibazilia on an e-mail,' she whispered. *'I had to do an awful lot of persuading for the e-mail to bring me up here. I really did miss Potatodai so much that I just had to see him.'*

Carrotpeaash and Turnipear both grinned. *'Tell the truth,'* Carrotpeaash scoffed. *'Tell the Princess why you are really here.'*

Princess Zamba directed her attention to Potatodai. He felt a slight chill go down his spine.

'So, Potatodai. What is going on? You did not tell me that your friend was coming here. If you had asked, I would willingly have given the go-ahead.'

One of the little pages ran in again and whispered something to the Princess.

'Snizzle, I do apologise. We seem to have run out of space hog juice,' she said. *'Instead, we can provide you with a little treat which will warm you up and also give you loads of energy. Eat two or three and you will feel fine.'*

'Okey dokey, anything you say,' replied Snizzlezallig. As she spoke, a trapdoor opened slowly above their heads and from it poured small coloured balls that looked like hairy marshmallows. They landed on a tray positioned directly below.

'Go on, eat them,' encouraged Potatodai. *'They are yummy. We call them Tukas. We only get them as a very special treat.'*

The Tukas were indeed delicious and much tastier than the finest soup Snizzlezallig had ever tasted from her cauldron. The outside tasted a bit like fudge and the inside like peanut butter, but they were soaked in a liquid that she had never tasted before.

Before she had even finished swallowing the second one she found her tiredness lifting and her energy coming back. Perhaps

Planet Zibazilia was not going to be the nightmare place she had thought it was going to be.

Having noticed that Carrotpeaash and Turnipear had left the room for a few moments to check on the wedding celebrations, Potatodai decided to speak. *'Your Sweet Highness, can I just let you know that I had no idea that this witch had planned on visiting me. It has come as a shock to me. I also have no idea as to what she is about to tell you.'*

Princess Zamba nodded. *'Please proceed with your story, witch. I am all ears. Zope, please get your quill and write down every single detail of the story. I do not want to forget even a word. I shall ask you to tear up the details if I think the story is in any way untrue.'*

Snizzlezallig began her story while Potatodai looked on in horror. *'Somebody is planning to overthrow our planet!'* Potatodai gasped.

He wondered if this ugly witch was telling the truth. If she was telling lies, then the bodyguards would punish her severely. Maybe this story was just an excuse so that she would not be punished for coming uninvited to Zibazilia! But deep down he was inclined to believe what she had said.

Princess Zamba continued to question her. *'It is strange how you should just arrive on our planet at the exact moment the conversation was taking place.'*

'It is strange indeed,' agreed Potatodai, *'but I can assure you, dear Princess, that this witch came here with only the idea of seeing me in mind. She did not come to make up stories. She even asked me to give her a kissy before I came back. Your Highness, I believe the earthlings do that when they are in a lovey-dovey mood.'*

Princess Zamba giggled. *'I had a feeling you were up to no good down on Planet Earth, Potatodai. Please continue with the story,* witch. *Afterwards, you can show us all how to kissy. It does sound like such fun.'*

Snizzlezallig proceeded to tell her story, and all those assembled listened attentively.

'A takeover of our Planet!' the Princess finally cried. *'Please call my bodyguards in here at once. Do you suspect any of our servants downstairs?'* she asked Potatodai.

He quickly shook his head. *'I have no idea who it could be. We will do everything in our power to find out who they are and to stop this awful takeover.'*

Carrotpeaash and Turnipear ran through the door at that moment. *'A takeover? Did we hear correctly, Your Highness?'*

The little Princess was wiping her eyes with a dainty strawberry hankie. *'It's true,'* she sobbed. *'I just knew it was going to happen one day.'*

Turnipear spoke first. *'We had a very small suspicion that something was going on, Your Highness. When you mentioned a trip to Planet Earth we were concerned. That is why we sent Potatodai, in the hope that he would bring us back an earthling. And that is why we did not go; we were terrified that something would happen while we were gone, and you had nobody to guard you.'*

A small pang of guilt overcame Potatodai. *'I'm sorry, Turnipear and Carrotpeaash. I had no idea. You knew that somebody was planning a takeover and you needed to hurry everything. Please accept my apologies.'*

Carrotpeaash continued: *'Let's not panic. Maybe we are over-reacting. Maybe aliens from another planet picked Zibazilia on which to have a meeting so it would be private. I will have a word with*

Kaoisa the space pumpkin later. He bounces his way around the sky all night and may be able to offer some advice and point out the traitors.

'We got a tip-off some months ago, Your Highness, but we thought it might have been nothing. Even so, we have kept our eyes glued on you ever since. That is why we were so annoyed when you snuck out through the back entrance to see Potatodai.'

Potatodai summoned his courage and spoke: *'Then again, everybody, maybe the discussion the witch heard referred to the takeover of another planet. How can we be so sure that it was ours they were discussing?'*

'Cause they mentioned the Princess,' answered Snizzlezallig.

'But maybe several other planets around here have their own Princesses,' said Potatodai, to which almost everybody nodded in agreement.

Four hours later they were still talking. Turnipear had started to weep. *'The thought of losing you makes me ill, sweet, sweet Princess,'* he confessed. *'I am sorry for making a fool of myself. Bodyguards should not cry. It is displaying a sign of weakness.'*

Princess Zamba offered him a rose-smelling hankie and gave him a giant strawberry smile. *'It is nice to know that you have feelings,'* she said. *'However, we must all work together on this. We must forget our differences for once and work as a team.'*

Carrotpeaash stood up and spoke. *'Maybe this witch creature was meant to pay us a visit. Without her overhearing this conversation, none of us would have realised how serious the matter was. It is true we had our suspicions, but by hearing about last night's conversation, it has made the whole thing very real indeed.*

'With your permission, dear Princess, we will ask your pages to prepare a very special meal for our guest of honour. Potatodai, you too are invited to attend the special celebrations. It is our way of saying thank you for going to Planet Earth.'

Princess Zamba nodded in agreement.

They ate and they drank, but they still had not reached a solution as to how to protect their beloved planet.

'We need to get help from somebody big and strong, like an earthling,' Turnipear stated.

Carrotpeaash scratched his anaemic looking head once again and opened his mouth to speak. He hesitated.

'Yes, Carrotpeaash, what is it?' asked the Princess. *'I can see that you are dying to tell us all something.'*

Carrotpeaash bowed and turned to face the assembled group. *'Well, it's just that, I know your mission to Earth failed, Potatodai, but please think again. Think again of a way to contact the earthlings and to bring one back here with you. Maybe together you and Snizzlezallig could find a way to bribe those e-mails to take you to Planet Earth again.*

'As for you, Snizzle witch, if you can help us to get Potatodai to Planet Earth again, we will find some way to reward you. Without you, we would not have known any of this. We will also wipe away any blame for you for coming here unannounced.'

Snizzlezallig heaved a big sigh of relief. Now she could get on with the job of getting Potatodai to fall in love with her. It might be a long wait, but she had all the patience in the world.

That night, Potatodai and Snizzlezallig walked together in the garden. Potatodai was on sentry duty. He had made a promise to Carrotpeaash and Turnipear that he would keep his eyes pealed for any unusual spacecraft circling around Zibazilia.

He was secretly happy with the unusual turn of events. Carrotpeaash and Turnipear had actually invited him to dine with them the following morning, and even better, they had invited Snizzlezallig too. Together, they would try to think of a way of getting immediate help from the earthlings.

'It's so nice that the bodyguards are looking for my help,' confided Potatodai to Snizzlezallig. *'This is the first time something like this has ever happened.'*

Snizzlezallig rubbed her rough hands together with great glee. *'Hubbildy bubbildy, ding dang gong, me feely an adventure coming on.'*

'Don't get too excited, Snizz; I am going to be telling Carrotpeaash and Turnipear that you are coming to Planet Earth with me. I don't know how but we will find a way–'

Snizzlezallig was having none of it. *'Hangy on now. An adventure for me means an adventure in the sky, not down on Earth.'*

Potatodai shook his head. *'You said you wanted to be with me, witch, so now is your chance. Take it or leave it. We will have to visit that little earthling in his wheelychair thingy. I think we can trust him and he may provide us with some more information. In fact, this time we may have to get to know his parents and ask for their help.'*

'You must be joking,' gasped Snizzlezallig in quite a state of shock. *'I already told you I can only go to Earth on Halloween night. I dropped you there last time because it was Halloween night. Earthlings get very suspicious of witches if they call around on other days. I will waity wait for you up in the sky.'*

'Okay, okay,' said Potatodai. *'You are probably right. I cannot afford to have you kidnapped by the earthlings. Right now, we need to find an e-mail who is willing to bring the two of us as far as the e-mail tunnel. From there, you will be able to use your broomstick again.'*

A strange shiver ran up and down Potatodai's spine as he suddenly noticed his witchy companion staring at him in the weirdest way. *'Oh no!'* he thought. *'I really hope she does not still fancy me. I thought after everything that has happened that we were friends. I hope she knows I would never go out with her. Maybe I could get her to fall in love with somebody else!'*

Even out of the corner of his eye, he could see her staring at him. It was all rather uncomfortable and something of a big mess.

Snizzlezallig was also thinking. She liked Potatodai, and she was determined that she would do anything to make him fall in love with her. *'A witch in love, oh my,'* even the thought of it excited her. She was going the way no other witch had gone before. She might even get herself thrown out of the Witch Society. However, more important matters were at hand.

Snizzlezallig had to do something to impress Potatodai. *'How are we going to get down to Planet Earth?'* she asked.

'We have no choice but to hitch a lift on another e- mail,' Potatodai said. That probably would work but it would not solve the problem of bringing an earthling back to Planet Zibazilia. No e-mail would carry an earthling. Firstly, they were far too large, and secondly earthlings kept the e-mails in jobs and it wasn't

the done thing for staff to kidnap their bosses and bring them to unknown planets.

Potatodai thought and thought. Both he and Snizzlezallig would have to befriend some of the passing e-mails and ask them to take them back down to Earth. They both knew how scared these little messengers were of their boss.

That evening, over dinner, Potatodai sought the advice of the bodyguards. He suggested that they offer the e-mails some sort of a bribe.

'And have you anything special in mind, Potatodai?' they asked. *'Yes,'* he answered. *'I have the very exact solution in my head.'*

'And what is that?' asked the bodyguards at once as they leaned forward to hear the answer.

'Why not offer the e-mails a small canteen at the edge of our planet where they can take a well-earned rest during their working day? Before they bounce off the sky they can have a few minutes to themselves.'

'Worth a try, as long as they don't come anywhere near the palace,' said Carrotpeaash while Turnipear nodded in agreement. *'And how do you propose putting this idea to the e-mails?'* they asked.

Potatodai thought long and hard. *'We will shout out our offer to a passing e-mail and ask him or her to take the message to their boss, Liame. I already invited Liame to Zibazilia, so this offer should really tickle his fancy.'*

'Nice one!' the bodyguards grinned. *'Please continue.'*

'In the message we will explain how a small canteen would provide a resting place for his e-mails on their long journeys. It would have

a few tables, and some light refreshments. This would make his staff happy and give them more energy, and therefore they will get their work done more efficiently.'

The evening ended with everybody happy and eager to put their plans into operation.

Two days later, the message got down to Liame by way of a passing e-mail and lo and behold, Liame agreed. There was one condition, however. Only senior e-mail staff, who would not use this as an excuse to doss, could give lifts. It would also be up to the individual e-mail as to whether they were in the mood to carry passengers or not. If they had a heavy load of a message then they were not to carry a passenger. Or if they were really tired and rushed, they could refuse if they wished. Only one journey a week up and down would be allowed, and only a small number of the same people from Zibazilia could only avail of the privilege. Liame felt that his e-mails should build up a relationship and a trust with the people who travelled with them. What would happen if a passenger threw one of their precious messages overboard?

Oh no, Liame was taking no chances on this one. Earthlings needed their e-mail messages and they needed them delivered fast. If they did not send e-mails, then Liame and his staff were out of business. What use was a stopover canteen on Planet Zibazilia if none of his e-mails had any messages to bounce to the top of the sky with?

Princess Zamba, Turnipear and Carrotpeaash held a farewell feast for Potatodai and Snizzlezallig that was fit for kings and queens. Some of the delicacies included stewed lip of a rare space fly called a zobat and roasted hairs off the tail of a space zobo, another much larger, but still rare, space beetle.

Potatodai beamed with pleasure. *'Maybe the bodyguards are finally beginning to trust me more,'* he thought. It then occurred to him that they may want to build up a friendship with the e-mails.

If his journey down to Earth was successful, they might bring
the Princess with them on a trip to Earth. They might even find
a hiding place for her there. Tensions were already beginning
to build around Zibazilia, as news of the overthrow spread
throughout the palace. Some drastic measures would have to be
taken, and quickly.

Princess Zamba came to the gates to say goodbye. *'Give the e-mails my good wishes,'* she said. *'I do hope one of them will be kind enough to stop. I will have someone check the edge of the planet every fifteen minutes to give me an update on your progress. I do hope you get a lift to Earth.'*

Carrotpeaash handed two bags of food to Potatodai and Snizzlezallig as they departed.

'Can I have the honour of shaking your hand, Potatodai?' asked Carrotpeaash. *'You are becoming something of a hero here, and we are proud of you. You have come a long way from being a sentry.'*

This request nearly made Potatodai faint. He quickly grabbed the bodyguard's hand and shook it ever so tightly. Carrotpeaash even hinted that Potatodai would have some nights off sentry duty every week on his return.

'Really?' gasped Potatodai.

'It is only because you are taking such a chance for our Princess,' he confessed. *'You have done more than anyone ever expected of you. You have impressed us. While you are trying to get to earth, we will weed out the spy in our palace.'*

Turnipear nodded. *'That is, if a spy exists, of course. I do hope you can find a way to bring an earthling up here, but the most important thing is to get the advice of the earthlings. Study their food and bring samples back if you can. It is possible that we may grow large instantly when we eat their food.'*

'*Or maybe we could plant some!*' suggested Potatodai wisely.

Potatodai was over the moon. For years and years, he had wanted Carrotpeaash and Turnipear to forgive him, and now it was happening. No matter what hardship he would suffer on the way to Earth, it would be worth it. He longed to be a respected member of Zibazilia once more.

He felt like dancing, jumping, and shouting with joy. He felt like singing a song with a hundred thousand verses that would never end. Life was better than it had been for ages. Now he had to put his full concentration into getting help and guidance from the earthlings. Things were so good today that he might even close his eyes and allow Snizzlezallig to give him one tiny kissy wissy, if it really meant that much to her. He didn't much like the thought, but he would put up with it.

'*Ouchy, what was that?*' yelled Snizzlezallig as she received a nasty slap across the ear.

A tiny space elf whizzed past her head, followed by several dozen smaller elves.

'*Gather around them in a circle,*' whooped the boss space elf. He was dressed from head to toe in green.

Potatodai turned around to face the newcomers. '*And what is the nature of your business, dare I ask?*'

Boss space elf pulled up one of his bright green socks and spoke in a clear and assertive tone. 'We are here on official business. We have heard that your Strawberry Princess has given permission for those e-mail freaks to have a canteen on your Planet. We would like you to know that the elf community is not happy.'

'*And may I ask the reason, please?*' asked Potatodai in great wonder.

'For years and years, we have pleaded with your two bodyguards to rent us a tiny bit of space so that we could play hide-and-seek between the rocks and they said no. No other planet up this far in the sky has tall rocks,' boss elf pointed out. *'We have decided to have a protest. Neither you nor that ugly thing with you can move until we have come to an agreement. Either those e-mails don't stop here or we get to play.'*

Potatodai sent a message with one of the runnerbean pages. Discussions went on in the palace for over an hour. Finally, the runner bean page arrived back with an answer.

'This is a message from her Royal Strawberry Highness, Princess Zamba of Zibazilia,' chirped the little page. *'It is with deep regret she has to say no one more time to the elves. You lot are too mischievous, she claims. You get up to too many tricks and you would be a bad influence on the junior Zibazilians.'*

'Fine!' roared boss space elf. *'Let her have it her way. Neither of these two will move from here.'*

By this time, two dozen more elves had arrived, and they had formed a tight circle around Snizzlezallig and Potatodai.

'Not too fast,' chirped the little page again. *'I forgot to say one thing.'*

'And pray, tell me what that is,' asked boss space elf cheekily.

The little page moved forward wearing a big smirk on his tiny runner bean face. *'You do remember that every single inhabitant of Planet Zibazilia drinks a glass of elf dew for their breakfast every morning, don't you? And that we purchase lots and lots of bottles from you lot?'*

'So?' answered boss space elf boldly. *'You can't get it anywhere else and you know it works wonders as an energy boost.'*

'So, yourself,' smirked the little page. 'I bet you didn't know that old Tonisa from Planet Tilahita has come up with a formula for a new drink that he says tastes nicer and gives more energy.'

'Nobody goes near those nasties from Tilahita,' answered boss space elf. 'The inhabitants of that planet are half man and half beast, and they have weapons hidden in their trunks.'

The little page stood his ground. 'One look at our beautiful Princess and everybody melts. Everybody loves and respects her, so going to Tilahita is not a problem. So, put that in your little green socks and smoke it.'

A moment later, space boss elf tied his little green cap, gave a quick nod, and all the elves disappeared into the sky.

Sadly, seven hours and three minutes later, Potatodai and Snizzlezallig were still sitting at the edge of Zibazilia, dangling their legs. E-mail after e-mail passed and refused to stop, as they bounced downwards from the top of the sky.

'We are only juniors and we are not allowed to stop,' said one lot.

'We are too busy, and we hate strangers,' said another few.

'We have just bounced off the top of the sky and we are building up speed, we can't stop,' was another excuse.

Boss space elf, who was feeling a little remorseful, sent his cousin over. His cousin offered to carry the stranded travellers two miles downwards, in the hope of meeting more e-mails as they slowed down. However, the little elf's legs buckled when Potatodai and Snizzlezallig clung on to his little shoulders.

'I'm really sorry. I would love to carry you, but you are too heavy,' he said sorrowfully.

The weary travellers decided to nibble some food and drink sparingly from their bottle of gnat juice. They wondered if Liame had forgotten their agreement. Of course, it was possible that none of the e-mails specially selected for the job were working today. Liame had made it clear that only certain e-mails could carry these special passengers.

Then suddenly, when they were about to give up hope, an e-mail screeched to a halt. He was puffing and panting, and seemed glad to have someone to chat to.

'Howdy doody,' he puffed in a deep, deep voice. 'Are you the two that have offered us a canteen and a rest stop?'

'We are,' shouted Potatodai.

The little e-mail puffed again. 'Are you going all the way to Planet Earth? If the answer is yes, remember that I can only bring you as far as the e-mail tunnels. If an earthling saw us taking passengers with their messages, we could be deleted.'

'Yesss!' echoed Potatodai and Snizzlezallig. 'Please give us a spin.'

'Hop on then,' said the panting mail, 'and do not forget to fasten your e-belts. My name is Employo. I've had a bad day and I am just so fed up with my job.'

'Why?' asked Snizzlezallig as she and Potatodai clambered aboard. 'I thought it would be very exciting paying visits to all those places with e-mail messages.'

'I'm the Work Mail,' explained Employo. 'I'm the one that's run off my feet. My job is all about those earthlings that are not happy in their jobs. They keep sending messages here and there, looking for new jobs. I no sooner arrive at my destination with one mail than I have to leave again with another. They apply for a job but when they go for an interview, they then decide that they do not want it. Off they go again, sending more and more e-mail job applications. They are never satisfied.

'I wanted to be the Christmas mail because then I would only have to work for about three weeks a year. But the boss wouldn't let me because I was not his favourite.'

'What about getting a helpy helper?' asked Snizzlezallig. 'My friend Gizo comes to Earth to help me on Halloween night.'

The little e-mail shook his tiny head. *'I told Liame that I needed a helper but he just won't listen. What can I do? I can't leave as nobody else would give an e-mail a job and I need the money.'*

Potatodai and Snizzlezallig both felt very sorry for him and told him that if they came up with any ideas they would let him know.

'Stop off at the new canteen to see me when I get back to Zibazilia,' said Potatodai. *'I will see what I can do.'*

'Thank you,' answered Employo. *'It is nice to know that I have some friends. Maybe some day you people might need some e-mail messages sent to other planets. So far, we only travel around Earth, but times are changing. We can have a chat about it sometime.'*

Soon they approached the e-mail downward tunnel.

'Let us outy here,' said Snizzlezallig. *'I can operate my broomsticky from here down to Earth.'*

Liame was waiting as they reached the tunnel. He had heard on the e-vine that Employo was carrying the first passengers downwards from Zibazilia.

'Oh, it's you again,' he said to Potatodai. *'Didn't we give you a lift up to Zibazilia a few days ago? At least we know that you are a trustworthy Zibazilian. By the way, is that canteen that you promised us ready yet? My mails are all excited about it.'*

Potatodai decided to be brave. *'Liame sir, the canteen will be ready in a few weeks, but I have another favour to ask.'*

Liame folded his arms. *'Shout it out, but don't think I am a soft touch either.'*

'Do you think Employo could have someone to help him? He is suffering from e-stress and needs a helper. I know it is none of my business, but he seems such a good e-mail carrier.'

Liame smiled. *'I admire you for your courage, alien, and I do think on this occasion I can help Employo out. I have noticed he is always on the go with very little rest. I will employ another mail to help him with some of his work. She will deliver all the messages informing earthling about interview dates. Employo can deal with the rest.'*

Employo arched his back with joy. He was so glad that he had picked up those two strangers in Zibazilia and given them a spin. They had brought him luck. His mother had always told him that one good turn deserved another. She had been so right.

'It would take the aliens to sort this out, wouldn't it,' he confided to a friend later on that evening. *'Just imagine, we couldn't sort it out ourselves.'*

It was Monday morning on Planet Earth and little Jason was fed up. *'I hate going to school,'* he told his mum for about the fifth time that morning. *'I cannot run and I cannot play football; I have to sit in this stupid wheelchair and watch everyone else. It's just not fair.'*

His mum was sad, but she was unable to do anything. She promised him a trip to the cinema that coming weekend and she promised him his favourite dinner when he arrived home from school. *'Roast chicken and roast potatoes,'* she beamed.

Jason wheeled himself into his bedroom. Even his toast and chocolate spread did not taste too good this morning. His school bag was lying on the bed. He suddenly remembered that he had not eaten his lunch on Friday and that the sandwiches were still in his bag. His mum would be so cross if she found out.

He decided to hide them under the duvet. His mum had already fixed up his bed so when he got home he could take them out again and maybe throw them out the window. The birds would love them.

'Come along, Jason,' his mum called. *'What is keeping you? You are going to be late.'*

'Coming, Mum,' answered Jason as he manoeuvred his wheelchair out of the room.

Little did Jason know, but at that exact moment, an e-mail had dropped two very important passengers at the opening to the e-mail tunnel. Seconds later they were whizzing down to Earth on the back of a broomstick.

Snizzlezallig had brought her broomstick to Planet Zibazilia but made sure it was folded up and hidden in her pointed shoe. Now she was back where she could use it again. Both she and Potatodai were exhausted. They had not had sleep for a few nights and all they wanted to do was to put their heads down for a few hours.

Snizzlezallig also wanted to go home to her den. She wanted to see Gizo, who by now would have organised a search party to scour the skies for her friend.

Yes, it was true they had loads of rows, but beneath everything, they were still great buddies. She had missed Gizo and was dying to tell her of her adventures.

The broomstick touched down at Jason's windowsill but to Potatodai's great disappointment the room was empty.

Snizzlezallig had broken out in a sweat because she feared she would be spotted by an earthling and possibly kidnapped. She quickly bade her farewell to Potatodai and told him that she would pop back from time to time to find out how he was getting on.

Potatodai was too tired to argue. His little eyelids drooped with exhaustion as he squeezed his way through a slight opening in the window. From there, he quickly jumped onto Jason's bed, under the duvet, and drifted into a deep, deep sleep.

He had another terrible dream. This time, Jackus Frostus had frozen him into a solid statue and all he could do was sit still all day while insects peed all over him and chipped at the ice all around him.

He also dreamt that Snizzlezallig had organised a secret wedding, and that he was destined to live his married life with her in the witches' den and be a guinea pig for magic experiments. Every time he had to do the kissy kissy thing with her, he threw up a few minutes later.

The day dragged for Jason at school until finally it was time for him to go home. He had been in a bit of a state all day. He hoped his mum had not found the sandwiches in his bed. She always got very cross if he did not eat proper meals. She worried that he would get sick. Maybe hiding the sandwiches had not been a good idea after all.

'What if she decides to change the sheets on my bed!' he thought. *'She sometimes does that on a Monday. What if the rotting sandwiches start to smell and she gets the pong as she passes his bedroom? Oh why, oh why did I not give them to the dog next door? He would have gulped them down in a second.'*

Once inside the front door of the house, Jason dropped his school bag in the hall and frantically wheeled himself straight into his bedroom. The thought of being grounded and not seeing his favourite television shows did not at all appeal to him.

His mouth opened in horror as he lifted the duvet and found that the sandwiches were gone. *'Okay, Mum,'* he shouted towards the kitchen. *'Tell me what my punishment is. Are you grounding me from the cinema? Are you taking away my pocket money? Or is it the TV?'*

'What are you talking about Jason?' his mum replied. *'Have you done something I should know about? Your favourite dinner will be ready shortly.'*

'Only joking, Mum!' he replied, laughing nervously. She must not have found the sandwiches after all. But if she hadn't found them, who had?

'Ouch!' Jason yelled, as he felt something at his ear. *'I have been bitten by something.'*

'Shh!' whispered a little voice. *'It's me, Potatodai, from Planet Zibazilia. Remember me? I am back, just as I promised. I have eaten the food that I found in your bed and I had a really good snooze – by the way, your beds down here are awesome, really comfy, if I may say so.'*

Jason was speechless for a moment. *'Is it really you?'*

'Yes, it's me,' Potatodai answered. *'Don't be frightened. Remember, I am frightened too. I am so little and you are so large. I have come here because I really do need your help.'*

'I won't harm you,' promised Jason. He hoped the little creature would not get sick from eating his stale old sandwiches. It would be a real problem asking the doctor to come and make an alien better. Even a spoonful of medicine would not fit in to this little creature's mouth.

'I need your help,' insisted Potatodai in a weak voice, *'because our Planet is in trouble. I have come to you because I think I can trust you.'*

'But I am In a wheelchair, and I am only ten years old,' croaked Jason, his voice hoarse with excitement. *'I am not sure how I can help you. I don't think I can even tell my mum or dad about you, so I will have to keep you a secret.'*

'That's okay,' answered Potatodai happily. *'I can live with that.'*

'So what's going on on your planet?' asked Jason. 'Is the Strawberry Princess unwell? What about those two horrible bodyguards?'

'Hey, hey steady on now,' laughed Potatodai. 'I can only answer one question at a time. My Princess is in a state of great distress. Somebody heard a secret conversation in the palace gardens about a plan to overthrow Planet Zibazilia. My Princess has sent me down to get help and advice from the earthlings.'

'Oh no!' gasped Jason. 'That is the most dreadful news. Are the bodyguards investigating?'

Potatodai stretched his little arms and sat up on the pillow. 'Actually, I have to take back what I said about Carrotpeaash and Turnipear. They have really changed and are making such an effort to be nice to me. When I go back, they have promised to relieve me of some of my sentry duties. I will have some spare time a few evenings every week. I cannot wait. There are so many games I would like to play. At least something good has come out of all of this.'

At dinnertime, Jason snuck little pieces of food up his sleeve when his mum wasn't looking. When he was finished, he said cheerily, 'I'm going to play some games on my computer, Mum. I have all my homework done.'

'That's fine,' she replied, happy to see Jason with a big smile on his face. Most nights he sat for hours just staring out the window at the stars and the moon. It was nice to see him doing something different.

'I will call you when I want to go to bed, Mum.'

'Okay, Jason, but don't leave it too late. Remember you have to get up for school in the morning.'

'Can I take a plate of choc-chip cookies to my room?'

'Of course you can,' his mother answered happily.

Jason chuckled to himself. Imagine if he told his mum that he wanted the cookies to feed a very hungry alien who was hidden under his duvet. She would definitely think he had gone a little potty.

Potatodai perched on the windowsill and together he and Jason stared out at the vast sky. Potatodai told his new-found earthling friend all about Planet Zibazilia. He explained how Princess Zamba would like the inhabitants of Zibazilia to be tall. He enquired about the food the earthlings ate and wondered if that kind of food would make his people grow and become strong.

Jason explained in detail to Potatodai what he, his parents, and his school friends ate.

Potatodai was intrigued. *'So, this must be what makes you big!'*

'I'm not sure,' answered Jason.

'If we could grow, then we would be able to fight our own battles,' confided Potatodai. *'We are so small that we would be overthrown in minutes.'*

'Then I think you may have to start using your brains instead of your hands,' answered Jason wisely.

Potatodai grinned. He was very impressed indeed. The little earthling was so right. They would have to use their brains to outwit their rivals. Even starting to eat an earthling diet would not make them grow overnight. He would need to do an awful lot more thinking. Princess Zamba always told him that he had brains to burn. If he had, then he would have to put them to use.

Later that evening, a strange pong wafted through the air and Potatodai saw the shadow of Snizzlezallig behind a tree. She was trying to get his attention by waving her broomstick.

He waited until Jason had wheeled himself in to the sitting room. *'Got to spend some time with the parents,'* he explained. *'If I stay all night in my room, they will begin to get suspicious. Just chill out for a while in my wardrobe and I will be back soon.'*

'Perfect timing,' thought Potatodai. *'Now I can see what my witchy friend wants.'*

'Are you okey dokey?' Snizzlezallig whispered loudly. *'I came down when it was nearly dark so nobody would see me. I was worried about you.'*

'I'm doing fine, Snizzlezallig. Jason is in another room but he will be back shortly. What are you doing here? I did not expect to see you so soon.'

'I know,' she replied, *'but I miss youuu and I can't stop thinking about youuu.'*

'Would she ever shut up with her silly notions, and think of a plan to savee Zibazilia?' he thought. *'The only reason she is hanging around is because she fancies me. But I need her to get me back to the tunnel, so I'll have to use my brains on her too.'*

'Come back tomorrow, Snizz,' he whispered loudly. *'Tomorrow we will talk. Jason will be back soon with his mum and dad who help him get ready for bed. Nighty night, Snizz. Sleep tight and give my regards to Gizo and the other witches,'*

'Night night, sweet pea,' hummed Snizzlezallig happily, as she disappeared into the night sky.

Soon it was bedtime. Potatodai squeezed himself into the back of the wardrobe as Jason's mum and dad kissed him goodnight.

Jason could not quite decide whether Potatodai should sleep on the pillow, under the duvet, or on top of the duvet. If he slept on the pillow, his parents might check in and notice him. If he slept under the duvet, he might get smothered. Finally, he decided that Potatodai should sleep under the duvet, but his little potato mouth should face towards the edge of the bed to breathe in fresh air.

'Are you asleep?' Jason asked seconds after Potatodai had curled up into a tight ball under the duvet. There was no sound, only the smell of roast potato as the bed became warmer and warmer.

Then, the worst thing that could happen happened. Potatodai started snoring. Jason was distraught. He could not believe that such a tiny creature could snore louder than a fully grown human could. He sounded like a train chugging up a steep hill.

'Shut up! The whole house can hear you snoring,' hissed Jason, shaking him as hard as he could. *'Shut up, I said.'* Jason had to give Potatodai one big pinch before he finally woke up.

'Me? Snoring? Never!' said Potatodai. *'Nobody has ever told me that before. If I am, I will blame the lovely soft bed that I am lying in. Now, may I please go back to sleep again?'*

Potatodai dreamt that he was six foot tall and twenty stone in weight. Together with an army of Zibazilians, he fought battle after battle against their neighbouring planets and won. He gained respect from everyone and Princess Zamba made him king.

It seemed as if he had only been asleep five minutes when Potatodai felt a tap on the shoulder. *'What is it now?'* he snorted. *'Do not tell me that I was snoring again.'*

'Wake up!' Jason yelled into his ear. *'I have to go to school. You will have to hide in the garden until I get back.'*

'No way,' answered Potatodai, wearing a big cheeky grin. 'Where you go, I go. I have had such a good sleep that I feel I can take on the whole world. You know that I have to find out information about how you earthlings live. I am coming to school place with you.'

'But you can't! My teacher would have a fit I brought an alien to class.'

'I'm not an alien, I'm a Zibazilian,' corrected Potatodai.

'Whoever or whatever you are, you just can't be seen around my school.'

'Then I will hide in your school bag,' giggled Potatodai.

'You can't stay in my school bag for hours. You would be so bored.'

Potatodai was not giving up. 'I promise I won't make a nuisance of myself. Can I please come? I might get some ideas when I see you earthlings together.'

Jason thought about it for a while. 'Okay, okay,' he agreed. 'But remember, if you get spotted you could be taken away and I may not be able to get you back. Nobody on Earth has ever seen a space person so they would use you for all kinds of experiments. I can imagine you in a glass jar, with people in white coats prodding and poking you and staring at you for hours. Then they might give you all kinds of tablets to see how you react to them. They already experiment on rats down here already.'

Jason felt so excited on his way to school. He held his school bag very tightly, smiling about his secret as Harry, one of the senior boys, pushed his wheelchair through the school yard. He was dying to introduce Potatodai to his teacher, but he knew he could not tell a soul. If he did, the newspapers would come to his school and those dreaded boring scientists come to take Potatodai away.

They might even take him away, too. Maybe someday, when he was bigger, he would tell the whole world, but for now this was going to be his secret. He was determined to think up a plan to help Potatodai and the little Strawberry Princess up at the top of the sky in Planet Zibazilia.

Tommy, the school bully with bright-red hair, was standing in the yard. His shoes were scuffed and his shirt hung out over his trousers. He looked as if he had already been in some sort of a scuffle. *'Here comes Wheelie,'* he jeered. *'He can't walk, he can't play football. He has to sit in that stupid wheelchair all day.'*

'Yep, look at him,' agreed five or six of Tommy's followers who had joined him.

'Here, let us give you a push down the hill,' yelled Tommy, looking around to make sure he had an audience. *'What d'ya think?'* he asked Jason in a sneering tone. *'Would you like to go for a spin?'*

Jason didn't answer him. Answering back only made Tommy worse. All that horrible boy ever wanted was attention. He was too frightened to tell his teacher about him, even though his mum and dad had advised him to go to the Head and complain.

'Teachers must be told about bullies,' they said. Jason did not agree. *'He will only make life harder for me if I tell on him,'* he said. His dad insisted that Tommy would be too frightened to do or say anything if he thought his teacher was watching him. Jason wasn't so sure.

'Well, wheelie boy,' taunted Tommy, quite delighted to see that a large ring of pupils had now come to watch.

Without a second's notice, Tommy landed head first into a large puddle of filthy water.

'Who did that?' he roared. *'I said who did that? When I find out, you are dead.'*

Nobody responded.

'Are you all deaf?' he screamed.

'We didn't see anyone go near you,' ventured a boy with thick glasses standing to his right.

'Then get your eyes tested, you nerd,' bellowed Tommy, shaking the dirty water out of his hair. He looked like a drowned rat crossed with a carrot. Several children tittered in the background.

'I know you couldn't have done it, wheelie boy, but someone else here is in very big trouble.'

Jason felt a tug from inside the leg of his trousers. Suddenly everything made sense. Potatodai must have got out. He was so small nobody would have noticed him. Jason remembered that Potatodai had told him that Zibazilians had super strength. He hadn't really believed him at the time, but now Jason sniggered to himself as he realised that Potatodai had indeed told the truth.

'That might teach you not to bully people, Tommy Shand – especially people who are less fortunate than yourself,' said a senior girl as she passed by. *'You are a disgrace and I'm glad you got drenched.'*

'Is that right, you nitwit?' shouted Tommy, not wanting to look even worse bad in front of the crowd. He opened his mouth and sent a big glob of spittle flying. It landed on the girl's school bag. *'That will teach you to keep your snobby nose out of my business,'* he jeered. *'And, by the way, that lip gloss you are wearing looks so stupid. You look like a sticky jelly bean.'*

Pumpkin Boy

Seconds later, Tommy's own face was completely covered in spittle.

'I'll get whoever did this. They will be very, very sorry. Nobody makes a fool of Tommy Shand, do you hear me?'

'Yes, we hear,' came a chorus of nervous voices. Everybody in the school knew how nasty Tommy Shand was.

Tommy dried himself as best he could, and slouched his way into the classroom shouting abuse at anyone who came near him. This had never happened to him before. He did not like being the laughing stock of the whole school. He could not quite figure out what the kid in the wheelchair had done, but Tommy had the strangest feeling that he was responsible. He would pay for that.

Teacher Tim droned on and on with his boring history lesson. 'Hands up who knows when the Second World War began.'

Jason's palms began to sweat as he heard Potatodai rustling about inside his school bag. *'He must be getting bored,'* Jason thought. He had come to get some ideas on how to save his planet and all he was listening to was stupid people talking about wars that happened years ago.

Potatodai wriggled out of the school bag and snuck up onto Jason's lap, under the desk.

'What next?' Jason thought. 'He is bound to be caught if he carries on like this.'

'It's all so interesting,' Potatodai whispered, much to Jason's surprise. *'I have learned such a lot in such little time.'*

'If you say so,' Jason answered. *'I'm bored stiff. I hate history.'*

'We don't have school in Zibazilia,' said Potatodai as quietly as he could. *'All we learn about is how to survive, how to read a little, how to make nourishing juices out of flying insects, and how to weave certain materials together to make our hammocks. We also learn how to squeeze each other's ears – we make juice from each other's ears.'*

Jason smiled. *'So that means that when somebody up there squeezes your ears, they have a potato and daisy drink!'*

Potatodai nodded. *'Correct, but there are many nicer drinks up there. One Zibazilian is made up of a coconut and raspberry. We all love to squeeze his ears.'*

Jason was enthralled. *'Wow! That is really something. I can't imagine squeezing anyone's ears around here.'*

Potatodai continued to whisper: *'We can read space script but we only own ten books in total. We are allowed to read only one page a month, so that we don't run out of reading material.'*

'Is everything okay, Jason?' asked Teacher Tim. *'Have you lost something? You seem to keep looking under your desk.'*

'I'm fine, teacher,' giggled Jason. *'My knees were just a bit itchy.'*

Lunchtime came, and Potatodai was very sad to see his friend sitting at the classroom window while all the other children went out to play. Now he understood why this little earthling was so sad; he was different from everyone else.

Jason recognised the look in the alien's eyes. *'Don't be sad, Potatodai. I sit here every day. I am quite used to it now. I just sit and watch everybody, or read my book if I wish. I am destined to stay in this stupid wheelchair forever and ever. I was born this way.'*

The class after lunch was maths. The bell rang, and children rushed in from the playground with red faces and dirty hands. Tommy had spent lunchtime thinking about how he would get his revenge on Jason. He saw the maths teacher approaching from the staff room. Now was his chance. He quickly grabbed Jason's school bag and scattered the contents around the room. Potatodai, who had gone back inside to hide, held on for dear life.

'See, everybody! He can't even pick up his books. Wait until teacher sees how stupid he is,' boasted Tommy. He continued to swing

the bag proudly over his shoulder while he beamed from ear to ear. It should not be long now until he was back in favour with everybody. But without warning, the bag became quite heavy, as if a big weight was pulling it down. And then, the bag banged against Tommy's face and his nose spurted with blood.

'Wha– what's ha– what's happened?' he asked in a dazed voice. 'Somebody give me a hankie!'

Everybody rolled around with laughter.

'Look, sir,' he yelled as the stunned teacher stood at the door. 'Look what they have done to me!'

The teacher had little – if any – sympathy for him. 'Well, Tommy, if you hadn't been up to mischief this would not have happened. You are always in some sort of bother. Do you think the teachers don't notice? Off you go now and when you clean your face give the bag back to its rightful owner. I don't have to ask whose bag it is, do I? Of course, it must belong to someone who cannot defend themselves. That's why you picked on them, isn't it?'

Tommy trudged towards the bathroom. His face was now almost as red as the blood pouring from it. Today just was not his day. Everything had gone wrong. Maybe he should ease down on being a bully for a while. He had not been getting that much attention lately anyway. His whole body trembled with anger. One of his own gang must be double-crossing him, but who?

Jason did not hear a word of maths class that afternoon. He just could not believe all the things Potatodai had done for him in the space of a few hours. He had a feeling that from now on, Tommy Shand would lay off. He could now go to school and that stupid bully would leave him alone.

'Now I must think of a way to help Potatodai's planet,' he thought. 'One good turn deserves another. Maybe being in a wheelchair is not too bad of a thing after all. If I was not disabled and had to spend my evenings indoors, Potatodai might never have come to visit me. Anyway, I will never know, will I?'

Potatodai slept on the windowsill that night. Even though the bed was so comfy, he had still felt a bit smothered the previous night. *'I rock myself to sleep in my hammock up in Zibazilia,'* he informed Jason.

'Won't you feel the cold?' Jason asked. *'Here, double up that cushion over there and wrap yourself up in it.'* But the cushion was too big and kept falling off the window, so Potatodai ended up sleeping on a few tissues.

'It's so nice to look up at the stars at work,' thought Potatodai. *'I wonder if they can see me down here?'*

His stomach ached and it gurgled a little because it was not used to such strange food. Slowly his eyelids drooped, and within a few minutes, he had gone in to a very deep sleep. It had been a rather exhausting but extremely exciting day. Tomorrow, however, the hard work began.

Tomorrow he would begin to research in detail the type of food eaten by the earthlings. He would also try to learn about some of the weapons they used in the wars they spoke about in class. He hoped the weapons might be small enough for him to carry to his home up at the top of the big blue sky.

Sometime in the middle of the night, Potatodai woke in a terrible fright. He thought he had heard a tapping sound at the window.

Jason had also heard the tapping. *'Who's there?'* he said. Neither of them could see anything but Potatodai knew exactly who was there. He recognised that smell.

'I'll go out and check. Back in a few minutes.' Potatodai opened the window, stood out on the ledge, and whispered loudly through the darkness. *'It's okay, Snizzlezallig. Don't be afraid. I think it is time I introduced you to my friend Jason. He will not harm you.'*

'Shutty gobby,' rattled Snizzlezallig. *'Looky uppy at the sky! There is something weird going on up there. I had to tell you.'*

Snizzlezallig was right. All the stars had assembled in the middle of the sky and had formed a very funny shape.

'They must be having a meeting,' thought Potatodai immediately. *'But why is Glitterati allowing them to do it at work? Something very odd is happening. I hope Princess Zamba is okay.'*

Jason, unable to get out of the bed without help, craned his neck to have a look. *'Please open the curtains fully, Potatodai. I heard you talking to the witch; tell her I won't harm her.'*

Potatodai did so, and after about a minute, the stars changed shape again. It was very intriguing.

'It's a message!' whooped Jason. *'They are sending you a message, look! The first shape is the letters ZA. The second was MB.'*

'But I can't read properly,' wailed Potatodai. *'The stars are far more educated than we are.'*

'I'm good at reading,' Jason reassured him. *'Let me do it for you.'*

The stars twisted and turned, turned and twisted until they had formed another shape. Each twist was a new letter. Finally, the whole message became clear. It told the sad story of the kidnapping of Princess Zamba of Zibazilia. Glitterati obviously had the brainwave of getting the stars to put the letters in the sky in the hope that Potatodai would see the message down on Earth.

Potatodai was devastated. *'That message is for me,'* he confessed. *'They want me to come back. I just know they do. Carrotpeaash and Turnipear need my help. What am I going to do? I have not gathered enough information.'*

'But the whisperers that night said it wasn't going to happen for two months!' cried Snizzlezallig, who had ventured onto the windowsill. *'I heard them say that the preparations would take at least two months.'*

Potatodai sighed. *'They must have changed their minds. I had a feeling we were being spied upon as we left. What do I do now? Do I stay down here and try and find a way of getting some earthlings to help us, or do I go back?'*

Jason was distraught. *'Does this mean that you are leaving already?'*

'For now, yes,' answered Potatodai, *'but I promise you I will be back. First, I need to go back and find out exactly what has happened. It is such a mess. My journey down here has once again been a waste of time. Goodbye, dear Jason. I will never forget you and I hope I will get the chance to come and see you again.'*

Jason was too choked with tears to answer him. Potatodai had sorted out the school bully and he did not have the time to sort out his problem for him. He felt like such a failure.

'Take me as fast as you can to the e-mail tunnel Sniz,' yelled Potatodai, as he jumped on to the back of her broomstick. *'And no going off course this time,'* he warned. *'It's an absolute emergency.'*

There was a smell of burning embers and a puff of dark red smoke as the broomstick gradually picked up speed.

'Where is Amouras, the Love Mail?' Potatodai asked the passing mails as they waited at the entrance to the mail tunnel.

'On a night off,' shouted one e-mail.

'Where is Porcha?' asked Potatodai. He also had the night off.

'Bambino, the New Baby e-mail, is coming. It's quiet tonight so he might give you a lift,' a passing mail suggested.

Bambino did stop, but he was quite reluctant at first, Then he decided that a bit of company would make the cold night go faster.

'Tonight has been very boring,' he yelled to his passengers as they both clambered onto his little back. *'Very few new babies have come into the world this evening, so I don't have to carry many congratulations messages.*

'I am not a senior e-mail, but under the circumstances, I am sure Liame will not mind me giving you a lift. A friend in need is a friend indeed, isn't that what they say?' he chirped.

Planet Zibazilia was in chaos when they finally touched down. Carrotpeaash and Turnipear were nowhere to be found. Heavy dark curtains covered the windows of Princess Zamba's chambers. Zibazilians stood here and there with their heads bowed. There was no music, only loud crying and wailing.

Potatodai shivered. This whole episode was a complete nightmare. *'Where are Carrotpeaash and Turnipear?'* he asked a page. *'I need to speak with them immediately.'*

'They too are gone,' sobbed the page. *'Somebody has kidnapped our Princess and Carrotpeaash and Turnipear. We are here without a leader. Somebody watched you leaving and realised that there was no sentry. They came in and took our Princess and her bodyguards away. We are all alone!'* he wailed. *'We asked Glitterati to send a message for you to come home. We thought you might be able to help us. Please try to do something. It is only a matter of time before the kidnappers come and take us away too. They are going to overthrow our planet,'* he sniffed. *'We are all doomed.'*

The little page was probably right. The threat was very real. Potatodai almost froze with fright even at the very thought.

'It happened when we were all asleep,' the page cried. *'We spoke to Glitterati and he said to bring you back, that you were loaded up with extra brains.'*

'Well isn't it nice to know that Glitterati and the stars care!' Potatodai answered in a caring tone.

The little page managed a weak smile. *'I'm glad you're back,'* he whispered, hoarse from crying. *'I will go and prepare some food for you, and for the Princess and Carrotpeaash and Turnipear, in case they escape and come back to us.'*

Potatodai wondered if it was it his fault for leaving the planet without a sentry. But on the other hand, he had gone to Earth to get help, and according to what Snizzlezallig had heard, the takeover was not expected for months.

He watched the witch as she stood hunched up into a ball in the background. She looked pretty miserable and frightened, and she was getting terrible looks from some of the Zibazilians as they passed by.

Snizzlezallig noticed Potatodai looking at her oddly. *'I hope they don't thinky I did it!'* she whimpered.

'Did what?' asked Potatodai.

'The kidnapping, of course. I hope they know that I'm a junior witch; I'm only allowed one small piece of magic every day and it doesn't work higher than fifty miles in the sky. Is this the price I have to pay for being in love?'

Potatodai tried his best to pacify her. *'There is only one thing we can do,'* he whispered in the lowest whisper possible.

'And what's that? It had better be good,' she answered sorrowfully.

'We will pay Jackus Frostus a visit. He is a real baddie. All he does is go around freezing everybody and everything. In winter, he even puts a mega long extension onto his spikes and freezes everything down on Planet Earth. I feel he may know something about the kidnapping.'

Snizzlezallig sat straight up in fright. *'Have you gone mad, Potatodai? We might be kidnapped too! Even we witches know what Jackus Frostus can do in the skyyy. One night last winter he froze the sky, and Gizo happened to be coming home from a party at that very minute. Her cape and sticky were frozen to the one spot until one of the senior witchies made a spell to unfreezy her.'*

'It's a chance we have to take,' said Potatodai sadly. *'Jackus Frostus may have nothing to do with the kidnapping, but he has a lot of enemies in the sky so he would be very happy to spill the beans on them if he knows anything.*

'I think when Jackus Frostus sees you he will get a fright. Just don't tell him you are a junior witch and that you are only training.'

'But our spells don't worky on him anyway,' answered Snizzlezallig. *'He is so ice cold that the spell would freeze before it ever got to work on him. And even if it did work, remember that we would have to get him down to Earth before my magic would work.'*

'Well don't tell him that,' warned Potatodai. *'Let us hope that he does not know any of that. We just have to go and see him. We don't have a choice.'*

Snizzlezallig shivered and slowly nodded her head in agreement. She understood that this was their very last chance. This falling in love business was hard work. Next time she fell in love she would make sure that it was with somebody closer to home, and somebody a heck of a lot less complicated.

Potatodai decided to ask Kiwiradish, one of Planet Zibazilia apprentice pilots, to take them on a short journey across the sky. He would ask him to circle around the cave of Jackus Frostus.

Potatodai knew that head pilot Aspalemon was a coward underneath, so he decided it was best not to ask him. He only went to Earth because Carrotpeaash and Turnipear had asked him and he was too frightened to refuse.

Kiwiradish agreed and decided that it was better to wait until the middle of the night to pounce on Mr Frostus.

'How do we know that he will be there?' asked Snizzlezalliq.

'That's easy,' he answered. *'Jackus Frostus only works odd nights here and there. He was out a few nights ago, so the chances are that he will not be out tonight. He stays in bed most of the time plotting and planning ways to freeze everybody out. His head is full of bad, bad thoughts.'*

Snizzlezallig then told him of another incident where Jackus Frostus had frozen a junior witch called Lidot to a wall. She had to stay there for hours and hours until Jackus went to bed, and the sun began to shine to melt the ice. She tried and tried her magic spells and none of them worked.

'Typical!' muttered Potatodai under his breath, *'just typical.'*

At approximately 3am, the Ziggercraft and its small crew went in search of Mr Jackus Frostus. He lived in a cave at the far top corner of the sky, so it was very easy to find. The colouring on that part of the sky was white instead of blue. It had become discoloured over time with the extreme cold coming from Jackus.

The Ziggercraft landed about fifteen feet away from his cave. Potatodai spoke in his loudest voice whilst taking cover behind the door of the Ziggercraft.

'Come out, you coward, come out now,' he yelled into the cave.

Jackus sounded very sleepy. *'Who's there?'* he asked in a deep, drowsy voice. *'I asked who is there and I need an answer, fast. You will be sorry for waking me. Nobody wakes Jackus Frostus.'* He was very, very angry.

'I think I will do a bit of flirting,' giggled Snizzlezallig, who had also hidden behind the door. *'It might soften him up a bit.'*

'Be careful,' Potatodai whispered back. *'He is a lot smarter than you think.'*

'What do you two want?' roared Jackus Frostus, peering through a slit in the cave. *'I can see through that door, in case you think I can't. Why can't I have a sleep without being disturbed? What exactly are you staring at, witch? Haven't you seen me in the sky often enough? I know all about you lot, with your silly spells and potions. You think you are better than anyone else. Ugh! The pong coming from you is making me sick.'*

'Well yesss, I have often seen you in the sky, Mr Frostus,' answered Snizzlezallig in a soft, flirty voice. She was getting a little nervous, since Jackus obviously knew more about witches than she thought. He had also stuck his scary icy head out of the cave.

'I never realised what a kind face and a lovely voice you had! I thought you were just veeery cruel, freezing everybody up. But then people with cold outsides often have very warm hearts,' she continued.

Snizzlezallig nudged Potatodai, making sure that he had noticed the pleased smile on the face of Mr Frostus.

'I only do what is in my nature witch and I am glad you realise it,' he snorted. *'You lot cast spells, don't you, and you are not scorned like me.'*

He glared at Potatodai as he rubbed a piece of ice off his spikes. *'Would you and your friend like to come into my kitchen?'* he asked. *'I have some bluebottle ice cubes if you would like to suck some.'*

'We will stay here, if you don't mind,' Potatodai answered. *'Our craft is very warm and comfy, and we are only passing through. Thank you for the offer of the ice cubes, but we are not hungry right now. We had some midge-ankle soup a little while ago.'*

'There's no one inside, if that what you're thinking,' said Jackus, as if he had read Potatodai's mind.

'I was not thinking that for a second, Mr Frostus,' answered Potatodai, who was stretching his neck from the door of the craft just to have a look. The cave looked miserable and freezing, with icicles hanging from the ceiling. Some of the icicles even had yellow mould hanging from their ends.

'I don't know how you sleep in such a cold place, Mr Frostus,' said Snizzlezallig, trying to make some more conversation. *'Then again, you are a veeery strong person. I bet you could live in any conditions, couldn't you?'* she giggled. *'I wish I was as strong as youuu. We witches have to speed around the sky to make ourselves warm. If we are not doing that, we are sitting around a big fire. It's terriblee to be such weaklings, isn't it, Jackus?'*

'Let's get out of here,' cried Potatodai sensing Jackus's anger rising.

'*You stupid witch!*' Jackus began to roar. '*I should have known you were making fun of me. I saw you look at that potato thing and laugh. You didn't mean any of those nice things you said about me.*'

'*Yes, I did!*' lied Snizzlezallig. '*I meant everything I said.*'

'*No, you didn't, you horrible witch,*' spat Jackus as he stuck out an extra spiky spike and punctured Snizzlezallig's long nose.

'*Come on, Snizz,*' yelled Potatodai. '*He's on to us! Let's shut the doors and get out of here fast. If he invited us in, then I think that he is has nothing to hide.*'

'*I don't know what your game is but whatever it is, I have done nothing wrong!*' Jackus bellowed after them as they closed the doors of the Ziggercraft and headed back for Zibazilia.

His voice was still booming as they took off. '*I know the Princess and her slimy bodyguards have been kidnapped,*' he yelled. '*I heard the rumours in the sky last night. I didn't do it! Why am I blamed for everything? Just because I have icy spikes? All that glitters is not gold, you know. Oh no, it's not.*'

Glitterati, head of the stars, had been listening to the commotion from a distance. He signalled the Ziggercraft to slow down as it approached him. *'Don't go there again!'* he warned. *'Leave it to me and my star staff. You two are not experienced enough to deal with brats like Jackus Frostus.'*

Potatodai was not too sure. *'What's the point in you trying?'* he answered in a weary voice. *'He invited us in, so the cave must be empty. We think Jackus is innocent. Somebody else must have kidnapped the Princess and the bodyguards.'*

'I will question him again,' promised Glitterati. *'Do you think Aspalemon had anything to do with it? I am surprised he did not come to help you today.'*

Potatodai hesitated for a second. *'I did not ask Aspalemon to pilot the craft. I do think he would not be able to cope if anything nasty should have happened.'*

Glitterati was not giving up too easily. *'Jackus Frostus knows what a bad temper I have if anyone tells me lies, so I will get the truth out of him eventually,'* he said with confidence. *'But if he did not do the kidnapping then we must find out who did, and we must find out quickly.'*

'Am I entitled to any peace?' growled Jackus Frostus, as Glitterati and two supervisor stars approached. He had just begun to doze back to sleep again. *'First it's that pongy ugly witch trying to play up to me with her pathetic sentry friend from Zibazilia, and now you lot.'*

'*Have you any idea who has kidnapped the Princess and the bodyguards?*' asked Glitterati firmly.

Jackus immediately went on the defensive. '*Why are you all picking on me? I already told the last pair that my cave is empty. Come, I will show you that I am telling the truth,*' roared Jackus.

'*No, no, no,*' replied fast-thinking Glitterati. '*You have taken me up all wrong. We are asking everybody, not just you. We are not picking on you. In fact, we were really looking for some guidance from you. After we leave here we are calling to all the adjoining planets.*'

'*Go along and annoy them then,*' blasted Jackus. '*I'm not guilty! Now let me sleep. I want to be wide awake tonight so I can freeze a few more earthlings down there, haha!*

'*Are you sure you know nothing?*' asked Glitterati once again, staring Frostus straight in the eye to see if he would flinch.

'*I told you so, didn't I?*' moaned Jackus. '*What do I have to do to get a bit of peace?*'

Glitterati and Siza, one of the supervisor stars, winked a star corner at each other. Neither had been mistaken. Jackus had twitched his left eye in a very nervous manner.

'*You seem to be on edge. Is something the matter?*' asked Siza, feeling courageous with his boss standing beside him.

'*Me? I am not on edge,*' growled Jackus. '*Nothing makes me nervous, especially you lot. You think you can come along and try to get me to admit to something I did not do. Well you cannot. Now, be off with you. I want to go back to sleep. Go and annoy someone else. I'm warning you now. If you do not, I will come and freeze you all to death when my body is frozen again. I know that I made an agreement never to do this to you stars, but you have really angered me.*'

Glitterati's face began to redden. *'Did I hear you threaten my stars?'* he yelled. *'I will give you one minute to tell us what you know, Jackus Frostus. If you do not tell us, I will gather up all the stars and get each one of them to turn on their lights. The lights will be so strong that you will be blind when they have finished with you, and the heat will stop you turning into ice.'*

'Shut up, you stupid star,' gloated Jackus. *'You call yourself the head of all the stars, Glitterati. Let me tell you what you are. You are a stupid nerd with nothing but stupid ideas, and you think you can frighten me with your stupid threats. You know very well the power of my icicles. Within two minutes, I will have zapped all the lights from your stupid stars. Think, and think carefully: if I can freeze all the planets in a few minutes, then what can I do to your stars?'*

'Don't even try, Jackus Frostus,' growled Glitterati. *'If you do, I will have a long chat with my friend Luna the moon. I will make sure that for the rest of your life he will never shine into your cave again. You will remain forever in darkness.*

'I will then have another quick word in the ear of my other friend Hapigleamatos the sun. I will instruct her never to shine into your cave in the daytime, so you will be in darkness both day and night. I know you are afraid of the dark. Am I right, Jackus Frostus? You answer me this second or you will be sorry.'

Embarrassed, Jackus answered in a deflated tone: *'I am afraid of the dark. I only go out to work when your stars are shining bright. I would love to know how you found out that information.'*

'Well?' roared Glitterati. *'Are you going to tell us all you know, or am I going to have to put my plan into operation?'*

Jackus thought for a few seconds. *'Okay, okay. I do know something,'* he confessed. *'I saw a craft from Planet Tilahita passing this way about the time your lot got kidnapped. I saw it landing over by the big rocks on Zibazilia and then seven or eight Tilahitans rushed in and I heard a lot of screaming.'*

'How did they get over the golden gate and the moat?' asked Glitterati. 'They would not have had a password.'

Jackus shrugged his shoulders. 'All I could see was something yellow on the ground, like a trampoline. They must have jumped on that and then bounced over the gate. One of them stayed behind and looked after the spacecraft. I could just see in the distance the lovely Princess Zamba and what looked like her two unpleasant bodyguards, the fat one, and the thin one, being dragged onto the Talihitan spacecraft.'

'Tell me more at once,' roared Glitterati.

'They were shouting and screaming. The Tilahitans must have made them reveal the password to the gate. The invaders had masks tied around their face and they looked as if they were carrying some dangerous weapons. They were all struggling, and the Princess was crying her eyes out. I must say I am a bit sad about the pretty Princess, but I cannot say that I am sorry for those two ugly bodyguards. They are always stuck to her like glue. Any time I wanted to say hello to her they told her to walk the other way.

'Anyway, the Talihitan craft was zig-zagging up and down and in the sky. I think they probably suspected that I was watching and they were trying to confuse me. They did not want me to know in which direction they were travelling. Now you know the truth, so be off with you. I am very upset about the beautiful Princess. It's just so unfair that everybody accuses me of everything!'

'Enough of the crocodile tears, Jackus Frostus,' said Glitterati in a stern voice. 'You must know that you have been causing havoc in the sky for years, and that is why we suspected you. It would have been easier if you had told this story to Potatodai and the witch when they asked you.'

'I was going to,' confessed Jackus. 'Then I caught the pongy witch mocking me so I decided I was not going to help her in any way. If Potatodai hadn't decided to desert the Princess, then it would never have happened, would it? He would have spotted the spacecraft landing and alerted the bodyguards. That's what a sentry does, isn't it?'

'We're truly very sorry,' said Glitterati, and he and his senior star hung their heads in shame. 'You just seemed to be the obvious person to blame.'

Jackus smiled and began to relax. 'I'm glad now that I told you. I was going to make you lot suffer by not giving this information. But remember, it is very easy to blame someone but make sure you check your facts before you do next time.

'If there is anything I can do to assist please call to me. Now I hope that is all the disturbances I will have for the day. I am looking forward to a long kip. Oh, I almost forgot, you must not tell the Tilahitans that I told you. They are half human and half animal and I hope you realise that they carry weapons in their long trunks.

'Long live the Princess!' shouted Jackus as they departed. 'Good luck with the rescue.'

'We were wrong,' admitted Glitterati to a senior star later that evening. 'We thought the look of fear it his face was guilt. We will make it up to him. It is awful to be blamed in the wrong.'

'Should we go to Planet Tilahita, boss?' asked the senior star.

'Await further instructions,' Glitterati said, as he prepared a hot drink of crushed gnat nails for both of them.

When Glitterati went home that night he was too upset to even think about sleeping. He even allowed his stars out in the sky without supervision. He decided to drink two large glasses of space dew, but that didn't even help. He tried counting the legs on the thousands of insects who were flying by, but that also failed.

When Thundrati, the maker of clouds, saw that Glitterati had not gone to work, he took advantage of the situation by making rain and making things blacker than they normally were. The stars that were working could not make enough light to outwit the clouds, so they gave up and went home early. Several of them had even refused to work that night because Glitterati had taken his bad mood out on them before he left. He regretted this very much the following morning and apologised to each of them.

They all understood when he told them how the inhabitants of Planet Tilahita had kidnapped Princess Zamba, Carrotpeaash and Turnipear.

The following day, Glitterati and Potatodai decided to hold a very important meeting with all the residents of Planet Zibazilia. Based on the information given by Jackus, and the conversation overheard by Snizzlezallig, they suspected that maybe one of their own people was a spy.

They agreed that all the Zibazilians would be asked a few questions in the hope that they would catch them out. However, the plan did not work. Everybody answered their questions correctly. The whole meeting had been a waste of time. They then decided to interview everybody separately, but this too proved useless. They then decided that maybe the Tilahitans had monitored the Planet for months and knew everybody's exact moves.

'Please be extra nice to Jackus Frostus, as we have accused him in the wrong,' Glitterati explained to everyone.

'There's no need for that, it was all a misunderstanding,' boomed a voice from behind. It was Jackus Frostus himself. He had heard about the meeting and stopped by to offer his help. Everybody was impressed and decided to think better of him from then onwards.

'As I see it,' Glitterati announced, *'we have no choice but to send Potatodai back to Earth. The earthlings are our last chance; without them, Zibazilia is doomed. Any day now, we can expect a takeover. I will have some of my stars do sentry duty while you are away, Potatodai, so let that not be a concern of yours. We hope that you will bring back some weapons that may help your people to defend themselves.'*

Glitterati also had plans for Snizzlezallig. *'Snizzlezallig will travel with Potatodai. If she assists in the rescue of our people, she will receive a very special space award. I will discuss that further with Old Man Time. A special reward will also be offered to any e-mail who transports Potatodai and Snizzlezallig. I will also encourage all my stars to be friendly to the e-mails.*

'Time is running out,' he warned. *'Spend as little time as you can down there but take any help which the earthlings are willing to offer us. In return, I will ask the stars to work extra hours so that the nights down there will not be so dark.'*

'Bravo!' shouted a rasberryprunewillow. *'Bravo! Potatodai will save our planet and bring back our Princess and her bodyguards. We will soon be one big happy family again. Long live the Princess and her bodyguards!'*

The meeting ended, everyone having agreed that Snizzlezallig and Potatodai should go down to Planet Earth again.

Snizzlezallig and Potatodai began their third journey to Planet Earth during a weekend, which proved to be a bad mistake as there were not as many e-mails around. The number of e-mails whizzing through the sky was halved because many earthlings were not at work and were not sending e-mails.

Snizzlezallig shivered as she and Potatodai waited and waited, and tried over and over again to get noticed by a passing e-mail. They saw the Date Mail passing by in the distance, but he thought that they were only waving hello so he waved back at them with one of his antennae and moved on.

Then the Sunday Dinner Mail sped past. He threw one look at them, threw his eyes up in disgust, and picked up speed. Hour after hour passed, and they began to get desperate.

Suddenly as all hope was fading, a very colourful mail slowed down for a minute to glance at them. Before he knew what was happening they had jumped aboard.

'Hey! Hey!' he shouted. *'Where do you think you are going? I am far too busy to give lifts. Your weight will slow me down.'*

'But, but, we have an agreement with Liame,' blubbered Potatodai. *'All senior e-mails are allowed to carry us down to the e-mail tunnel. That is why we have provided a stopover canteen for you up here.'*

'Do you know who I am?' asked the e-mail, trying to make room for everyone. He answered without waiting for an answer. *'I'm Aegio, the Birthday Mail, and I have a hundred and one different birthday greetings to deliver.'*

'*Do you know Amouras? And Porcha? And Politico?*' asked Potatodai.

'*Of course I know them,*' he answered drily. '*We have dinner together most nights.*'

'*Well we are friends of theirs,*' Potatodai informed him. '*They helped us out in the past.*'

A little smile brightened Aegio's tiny face. '*That's different! Anybody who is a friend of theirs is a friend of mine. I have worked with them for six years and we are great buddies. They are always there for me when I need a friend. Welcome aboard.*'

Jason was fast asleep when Potatodai landed on the windowsill. He was having a very weird dream, in which he had borrowed a wand that belonged to Snizzlezallig. He brought the wand to school and turned that bully Tommy Shand into a slimy green lizard with one purple fang and one yellow one. Everywhere he went his slime stuck to things. It was all over his desk and his schoolbooks.

Then, when that fun was over, Jason waved the wand again and this time he turned him into a two-humped camel. Poor Tommy was too tall to fit through the door of the classroom as his humps kept getting stuck. Jason was the new class hero, and everyone wanted his autograph.

He woke with a jolt when he felt someone tapping him on the shoulder. '*Get away, Tommy Shand!*' he cried. '*I didn't mean to turn you into a camel.*'

'*Shh!*' whispered Potatodai. '*It's only me. I have come down again as we are in such terrible trouble.*'

'*Is this another dream?*' Jason mumbled in a sleepy voice. '*What's going on?*'

'No, it's really me, your friend Potatodai, and I really do need your help. This is my third visit to Earth and this time I must go back with some sort of real help.'

'I had a long think about this, and I am not sure how I can help,' Jason sighed. 'We earthlings are far too big to travel up to you and our planes only go up a few miles in the sky. I don't want to ask my Dad because he might insist that you stay down here.'

Potatodai nodded. 'I know you are only ten and that you are not able to walk, but you have lots and lots of brains and I think you can give me some ideas for how I can save our planet. I'm sorry I had to leave so quickly last time, but the Princess and Carrotpeaash and Turnipear were kidnapped. The Tilahitans came and took them away and now we are in fear of being taken over.'

Jason rubbed his eyes. 'Is the witch with you? I can smell a hint of her funny smell.'

Potatodai yawned. He had been having so little sleep lately. 'Snizzlezallig has gone back to her den but she will be calling later to see how I am getting on. Let me have a few hours' kip and I will tell you all about it during your school break tomorrow.' The smell of fried potatoes filled the air as once again Potatodai fell into a deep, dark sleep.

Jason was chuckling so much on the way to school the next morning that his dad asked to know what was so funny. 'I'm just thinking about a slimy lizard and a two-humped camel,' he giggled, offering no further information.

He felt happy and confident with Potatodai safely tucked up in his school bag. He felt he could take on the world knowing his little friend was with him. He had one idea up his sleeve as to how to help him, but they would discuss it later. And perhaps the alien could help him too. Tommy the bully had started to play up a bit again, and Jason hoped Potatodai would teach him another lesson.

'First class is science,' he explained to Potatodai. *'I want you to stay very still. I hate science, so I must make sure I do not get on the wrong side of my teacher. Things will only get worse if he has a pick on me.'*

Potatodai had not heard a word Jason was saying. He was in a deep sleep, tucked up in the school bag hanging at the back of Jason's wheelchair. He too was having a weird dream.

Potatodai was dreaming about Jackus Frostus. His cold spikes had turned to jelly, which attracted all the insects in space. They came and ate the jelly, and Jackus was left with no spikes. Then he dreamt that Snizzlezallig had tricked him into getting married – a dream so awful that he woke with a jolt. He could not remember where he was for a second and he panicked. With his great strength, he gave one huge push to the wheelchair.

'Stop it! Stop it, Potatodai!' Jason hissed, hoping that nobody in the class had heard him. Nobody had heard him, not even Potatodai, who still thought he had got married to Snizzlezallig the witch. The wheelchair raced with alarming speed up through the classroom and straight over the feet of the science teacher, who screeched in pain.

'Have you gone mad, Jason?' the teacher roared. 'What do you think you are doing?'

But the panicked Potatodai still had not woken up properly and he continued to push the chair, which moved out through the half-open classroom door and down the corridor towards the principal's office. Everybody in the classroom roared with laughter and the science teacher just staggered helplessly down the corridor after them.

Miss Tansin, the school principal, was in a bad mood. She had been up half the night with a new puppy that wouldn't stop yelping and going to the toilet on her good rug.

'What on earth is going on?' she asked, with a dismayed look on her face. 'Jason, come into my office this instant.'

She could see the science teacher in the distance, hobbling down the corridor with a pained look on his face. *'Call the doctor. I think he broke my big toe,'* he moaned. *'That boy must be punished.'*

They whispered together for a moment and finally Miss Tansin asked a passing teacher to bring Jason back to his classroom again. *'You are not allowed to play pranks in the classroom,'* she said. *'Your parents will be hearing about this.'*

'Totally out of character for that child,' he could hear her saying to the people in the staff room as he was wheeled away. *'I cannot understand what came over him. He is normally such a sweetie.'*

'Sorry, Jason!' whispered Potatodai, now fully awake in the bag. *'I completely forgot where I was, and I panicked.'*

But even though Potatodai was now awake, he was still in a mischievous mood. The sleep had obviously done him the world of good. This time, however, rather than embarrass Jason, he was determined to make him laugh. He would desperately need his help after school, so he wanted to make sure they were still firm friends.

At the break, Potatodai crept out of the schoolbag and hid in a large rubber plant on the corridor directly outside the classroom door. Then the fun began. Each time the door was opened the leaves of the plant began to shake and rustle and boogie in a crazy fashion. When a person passing by turned around to look, there was silence. When they started to walk away again, the noise began again too. All the passers-by scratched their heads and blinked in amazement – some even cleaned their glasses. They then walked away in a big hurry in case anyone would see them acting so strangely. At one point, a teacher did lift one of the leaves to investigate but decided there was nothing there and walked away. *'Phew! That was a close one,'* thought Potatodai.

'I should really stop taking such chances. These earthlings might not all *be as nice as Jason.'*

Jason had watched the whole carry-on and he laughed so much that he forgave his little friend immediately. He rang his mum and told her he had decided to wheel himself home from school. *'It will tire you out,'* she warned. *'You will not be able to do your homework.'*

His mum's words were ignored; these few private moments with his guest were ever so precious. Jason knew from experience that his alien could disappear at very short notice, so he wanted to enjoy every single moment that he had with him.

Jason's dad and mum were not too happy when he finally arrived home. He could hear his mum's voice before she even opened the front door for him.

'What's going on, Jason? First you decided to wheel yourself all the way home and then we get a call from your head teacher?'

'A call about what?' asked Jason, trying his best to put on an innocent face.

Miss Tansin had made the telephone call before Jason got home, and had complained bitterly that he had been playing practical jokes. *'He wheeled himself at speed through classroom, over the teacher's toes, and up the corridor. And he acted strangely for the rest of the day.'*

'How could my son possibly wheel that chair that fast?' argued his mum.

Miss Tansin was not in the mood to discuss the situation, and asked his mum to ensure that it would not happen again. Potatodai was very unimpressed when he heard what the headmistress had done. She had no right to upset his friend.

Jason pleaded with him to understand, but Potatodai would not listen. *'Nobody squeals on a friend of mine!'* he warned. *'She will pay for this.'*

Jason decided there was no point in arguing. He just hoped that Potatodai would not go too far and that somebody would find him.

He and Potatodai chatted in bed for hours and hours that night. Jason put forward a few ideas but every time Potatodai shook his head. Snizzlezallig paid a visit but was sent home until the next day.

The next morning arrived quickly and Jason prepared for school. Before he left he promised his mum that he would be good and would not get involved in any funny stuff. Potatodai clung tightly to the inside of his school bag and off they went.

Today Jason was having that stuff called cheese and ham in his sandwiches. Potatodai decided to have a chomp of them, as they looked so tasty. He was sure Jason would understand. Jason met Miss Tamsin on the corridor and she beamed a nice good morning at him as she passed. She seemed to have forgotten yesterday's incident.

But Potatodai had not forgotten, nor had her nice smile made him look any differently on the situation. During the eleven o'clock break, he crept silently out of Jason's school bag and hid inside a lampshade on the corridor. When the break was over, and the teachers had gone to their classes, he ran at tremendous speed along the corridor. He made his way into the empty staffroom. There were many handbags and briefcases lying around, so it was hard to figure out which one belonged to Miss Tansin.

There was one clue; he remembered that yesterday she had been chewing what earthlings called a 'pastry'. She might have another one today. Yes! The black briefcase sitting on the desk in the corner had a see-through bag in it that contained the exact same pastry as yesterday. It had to be hers! The briefcase was stuffed with papers. One bundle of papers took his notice; it had loads of red markings. These looked like the kind of thing he could have fun with. He took each of the exam papers and he nibbled away the middle of the page. He left them in a terrible state. *'That will teach her,'* he thought. *'Nobody complains about my friend Jason.'*

Potatodai swiftly edged his way out of the staffroom. His mouth was dry and tasted like paper. He longed for a drink. He suddenly noticed Tommy Shand coming up the corridor. He quickly hid behind a large bin and as Tommy passed, he gave the bin a large push and held on to the bottom of it. Tommy nearly dropped his pants with fright when he saw the bin coming at him. His face was redder than his hair and he didn't look back once as he sprinted to his classroom.

The bully dropped his lunch as he ran and so Potatodai enjoyed a ham, mayonnaise and crisp sandwich as he clapped himself on the back for doing such a wonderful morning's work.

His little heart still tinged with sadness, however, as he thought of all the things which were happening on his own planet. Earth was fun, but his job was to save his own people. He had to act quickly or he might have no planet to go back to.

Meanwhile, Jason's brain was working overtime. He had not heard one word the geography teacher had said. He was lucky he had not been asked any questions. He, too, was aware that time was running out up on Planet Zibazilia. One idea had entered his head, but he was not sure what Potatodai would think of it. He would tell him after school.

Potatodai was intrigued when he heard the plan. *'You think I should put on a disguise and go over to Tilahita to rescue the Princess! But if they found out it was me they would kidnap me too!'*

Jason was not even listening. He was already wheeling himself towards his wardrobe.

'See that big bag over in the corner? Pull it out please.'

'Why! What's in it?' asked Potatodai.

'You'll see,' smirked Jason. *'I am about to give you a brand new image.'*

Potatodai placed the bag on Jason's lap. Out of it came lots and lots of Jason's baby clothes.

'My mum kept them all,' he laughed. *'Aren't they cute? Let's try them on you. First, we will have to cut off some of the daisies off your face.'*

Potatodai couldn't quite believe that he had agreed to this. *'I'm not happy to lose my daisies,'* he confessed sadly. *'But, if this helps my Princess and my planet then I will do it.'*

the maid e-mail

After a lot of chopping and wrapping, the job was complete, and Potatodai found himself wearing a bright blue baby suit with a hood.

He had blusher on his cheeks that Jason had taken from his mother's make-up bag in the bathroom. Jason completed the look with a big dab of bright red lipstick.

'Have a look in the mirror,' giggled Jason.

'I'm bald!' screeched Potatodai. *'All my daisies have gone. I don't know this stranger in the mirror.'*

Potatodai took another long look. Finally, he shrieked with delight. *'It's brilliant! Nobody will recognise me, so I can go to Planet Tilahita and have a good snoop around. If anyone asks who I am, I will tell them that I am from a planet hundreds of miles below them and that I am lost. I can always grow my daisies again once I have rescued the Princess and the bodyguards.'*

Jason beamed with delight. *'Glad to be able to return the favour, Potatodai.'*

'You are only ten, Jason, and you are such a genius!'

As well as fashioning his disguise, Jason had arranged some tools for Potatodai. That morning, over breakfast, when his mum wasn't looking, Jason had hidden lots of things in his wheelchair, including a cheese grater, some Rice Krispies cereal, some milk, glue, a mouse trap and a few more household utensils. *'Don't tell Mum,'* he whispered to Oxo, his big black cat, who was staring at him with her big green eyes. He wrapped the bits and pieces in a tie-string laundry bag that was almost bigger than he was.

Finally, Jason asked, *'Please take Oxo, my cat. I think he may be able to help you.'*

Oxo, on hearing his name, made a dart for the window and disappeared. He was going nowhere that might not have milk.

It was a very worrying few hours for Potatodai and Jason, as they waited to see if Snizzlezallig would turn up. But true to her word, she tapped lightly on Jason's window at a quarter after ten.

'Cooeee! Are you ready?' she whispered. Gizo was with her on another broomstick.

Jason was fascinated. *'Hello, witches!'* he beamed. *'So many things have happened to me lately. First I meet an alien and now I get to meet two real witches.'*

'Hellooo!' they replied in rather frightened little voices. Both witches appeared a little nervous of Jason. They knew that they were not welcome on Earth unless it was Halloween.

'What on earthy have you done to yourself, Potatodai?' asked Snizzlezallig, throwing him an admiring glance. *'You have a completely new image. You look a million dollars.'*

Gizo had to agree. *'Jump onto my stick,'* she shouted. *'You have never had a spin on my sticky wicky.'*

'Leave him alone,' yelled Snizzlezallig.' *I thought we had all this business sorted out. He is my friend and not yours.'*

'Okay, okay,' agreed Gizo. *'He is your friend, but pleasy, pleasy, pleasy can he go half the way on my broomstick.'*

Snizzlezallig agreed reluctantly. *'When you get to the e- mail tunnel circle around and waity for me to get there.'*

'Okey dokey,' cackled Gizo.

Snizzlezallig was suspicious. She wondered what Gizo was up to but she decided to give her a chance.

Potatodai promised faithfully to have the stars send a message down to Jason. *'They will weave a message all over the sky for you. No matter what happens, we will let you know what is going on.'*

Gizo and Potatodai sped away into the night, leaving Jason sitting at the window in his wheelchair, looking up in to the night sky. Snizzlezallig blew him a kiss and flew off behind them. She knew she had no chance of catching up with Gizo; Gizo had a black and white broomstick, which had much greater speed than her mustard-coloured one.

Jason felt ever so proud. It was hard to believe that he was the only person in the whole world who even knew that Planet Zibazilia existed. On top of that he had thought up a plan to help save the Princess. He really, really hoped it would work.

Up in the dark night sky things were not at all going according to plan. Snizzlezallig lost herself in a daydream for a minute, and when she turned around Gizo was gone, and she had taken Potatodai with her.

'*Well, the nerve of her!*' bawled Snizzlezallig to the night sky, and to anything that was willing to listen. '*I knew she was jealous of meee but I never thoughty woughty that she would play a trick like this on me!*'

She circled and twirled at great speed around the sky, but both Gizo and Potatodai had disappeared. Gizo would be sorry. It was the last time that she would double-cross Snizzlezallig.

Snizzlezallig begged and begged for a meeting with Liame. After three quarters of an hour, he finally appeared.

He had obviously been eating, as he burped as he spoke. '*What do you want, witch? You've been hanging around here a bit too much for the last few weeks. What are you plotting, warty face? Have I not done enough for you and that alien friend of yours?*'

'*Did any of your e-mails give a lifty in the last hour?*' she asked in a low voice. Her lips were trembling with fear; she was not used to being spoken to like this.

'*No, they didn't,*' Liame burped. '*I haven't seen anyone strange around the tunnel all day.*'

'Hello!' sang a musical voice. The cutest little cherub in the whole universe had just appeared out of nowhere. She glittered and sparkled and shone every so brightly.

'Hello little cherub,' answered Snizzlezallig.

'I have some news,' sang the cherub. 'I want to know if it's love. If it is love, then I need to find Cupid, because Cupid will cement that love and draw the couple closer together.'

'What are you babbling on about?' asked Snizzlezallig. 'You are singing in riddles.'

The cherub adjusted her halo. 'Gizo is hidden over there in a dark cloud,' she giggled. 'I think she has a lover with her. She is doing her best to get a hold of him. Love is such a wonderful thing. I do hope it will all work out.'

'Not if I have anything to do with it,' confessed Snizzlezallig. 'That spud is mine and mine only. I will fight to the bitter end to get him. Get out of my way, cherub. Keep on singing but remember, nobody tries to steal my spud and gets away with it. You can tell Cupid to go back to sleep – it ain't happening.'

The little cherub was right. Gizo and Potatodai had stopped in the middle of the dark cloud. Snizzlezallig rushed over.

'I don't have anything to say to youuu, Gizo,' cackled Snizzlezallig. 'Actually, I dooo. I disown you as a friend.'

'Now, now, ladies, please!' cried Potatodai. 'I am not worth a row.'

After a small struggle, Potatodai changed broomsticks, and he and Snizzlezallig finally arrived at the e-mail tunnel. Snizzlezallig had said that it was too risky to go up to Planet Zibazilia, but she suddenly changed her mind.

'I will come up with you and try to help,' she squeaked in a weak voice. *'I am sooo ashamed of what my friend did. I don't care if I get kidnapped.'*

'I would dearly love you to come. You can help me carry the bag that Jason gave me,' said Potatodai.

This time they were lucky. They were only waiting for fifteen minutes when Amouras, the Love Mail, stopped with them.

'Hop aboard,' he called. *'You'll have to excuse me this time; I'm not in the mood for chatting. Two of my customers have fallen out and they are not in love anymore. I have had to deliver two messages breaking off romances. That makes me so sad. I loved carrying their lovey-dovey e-mail messages. It made me happy to see them so happy.'*

As it turned out, nobody said a word the whole way to Planet Zibazilia. Each was lost in his or her own thoughts and worries. On their arrival, Amouras skidded to a halt behind a large, jagged rock.

'You two are up to something,' he joked. *'You have a very suspicious look. I'm off, before you drag me into trouble. Toodle pip!'*

Aspalemon the pilot had spotted their arrival and made his way towards them. *'Is it really you?'* he asked in astonishment.

'Yes, it's me,' Potatodai chuckled. *'You can stop squinting your lemon eyes at me.'*

'I am so happy to see you, Potatodai,' he exclaimed. *'I know I don't know you that well, but I know very well how badly everyone missed picking your brains. Glitterati, Glitterati!'* he shouted across the sky. *'Potatodai is back. You told me to call you when he got back. You won't believe what he looks like! I only recognised him when I smelt his potato smell.'*

Glitterati shot across the sky. He wrapped his star points around Potatodai with joy. *'I was so worried,'* he said. *'I thought you might not come back.'* He gave Potatodai a once over and laughed. *'I love your disguise. I hardly knew you. Is that an earthling costume you are wearing?'*

'It's called a babygro,' Potatodai chortled. *'Newborn baby earthlings wear them. In fact, most of the baby earthlings are larger than we are. Isn't that something! Is it any wonder that dear Princess Zamba wanted help from the big strong earthlings?'*

But Glitterati was not in the mood for jokes. *'Aspalemon and I have had a long talk and we feel it is time for one of us to visit Planet Tilahita.'*

Potatodai yawned. *'Why do you think I came back from Earth dressed in this disguise?'* he asked. *'I was thinking ahead. I am ready to visit Tilahita.'*

'*Well you will have to come up with a pretty good fib,*' Glitterati and Aspalemon agreed.

'*Oh ye of little faith,*' laughed Potatodai. '*They don't call me a brain box for nothing. I have a plan.*'

Aspalemon boarded the baby Ziggercraft while Potatodai gave Snizzlezallig her orders. '*You are the Zibazilian sentry. If we do not come back within five or six hours, please call Glitterati and tell him we need help.*'

Snizzlezallig tensed her shoulders She knew that she had little choice, but she was scared. '*What if the kidnappers come back and take meee?*'

Potatodai thought he would try to comfort her. '*No offence, but you look strange and scary. One look at you and the kidnappers would run a mile!*'

The ground on Planet Tilahita was very rough and the air was chilly. Tiny fragments of glittering stones stuck out of the ground like sharp daggers. Even though there was nobody about, there was an eerie feeling of eyes watching from everywhere. There was a loud clanging noise – probably the sound of weapons being polished, thought Potatodai to himself.

'I will wait for you in the Ziggercraft, as I don't think it is safe to land anywhere here for too long,' whispered Aspalemon, wiping a bead of sweat from his forehead. *'Please be confident in the knowledge that I will be here to take you back. I wish you the best of Zibazilian luck.'*

'Yes!' agreed Potatodai. *'It is a very good idea to split up. At least if I am captured you will be able to go back to Planet Zibazilia and get some help for me.'*

'Well my thinking was a little different,' confessed Aspalemon. *'I was afraid that if I hovered in the air they might recognise my craft and they might shoot me down. I will leave the craft on the ground until I am forced to take off. Whether it is true or not, I am led to believe that the Tilahitans are armed. We cannot afford to take any chances.'*

The reality of the whole situation only now began to dawn on Potatodai. He had heard this rumour before, but he did not believe it. He longed for his cozy hammock and a glass of fizzy space dew. Even sentry duty seven nights a week was better than this mess.

Potatodai checked to see in which direction the main Tilahitan village lay. His babygro suit was very hot and itchy but he plodded onwards. He wondered if he was too late. Maybe the Princess and her bodyguards had been killed or become slaves. If it was not too late then everything about his visit to Planet Tilahita must go well. He could not afford to make a single mistake.

It took Potatodai quite a few minutes to tramp his way through the sharp-edged stones. He wondered if the creatures here had padded feet. Nobody could walk on these stones every single day.

Closer to the main village, groups of Tilahitan sentries with long trunks stood here and there. Their faces all strangely resembled the earthlings' faces in one way or another. The only difference was that the Tilahitans had trunks. The rest of their bodies had descended from animals.

Nobody asked Potatodai his business, but as he passed, each of the sentries wiggled their trunks and spoke to the next one through a headphone on the side of their tongues. The words were in code and sounded like *'PING, PINGY, PINNNGGGYYY, PUNG, PUNGY.'* It was all very frightening.

Finally, Potatodai arrived at the main entrance to the Tilahitan palace. It was very different to the palace in Zibazilia. This one was ugly and it looked like it was made of pieces of steel overlapping over each other. Between the steel pieces were small peepholes.

Potatodai was by now feeling very, very warm and he longed to get rid of the stupid babygro suit. 'What are you thinking, stupid?' he asked himself. 'You have come in disguise and that is the way you are staying.'

At the second set of gates, he was questioned in detail by a rather stern-looking sentry who looked like a rhino with a hole in the side of his face. It became clear that the trunks could be folded up and drawn into the face.

'Can I have a private word with your ruler?' Potatodai asked.

'Bout what?' snorted the rhino, spitting some yellow and red space grass into Potatodai's face. 'What's your business, freak?'

'The matter is one I do not wish to discuss in public,' Potatodai answered. 'Please tell your ruler that it is of the greatest importance.'

Once again, the sentry consulted a colleague and he allowed Potatodai to move a little further into the palace. Finally, he arrived at the heavily guarded door of the ruler, Hermiza. By this time, two armed sentries walked in front of him and two behind. These four had bulging trunks and they smelt of gunpowder.

Potatodai was too scared to even blink. He told himself not to think about what they had hidden in their trunks. He would have to confess his business before he was allowed to meet Hermiza. He knew he could go no further otherwise.

'Please tell me your name and from where you have come,' roared another sentry, who came to the door in full uniform. 'You will not be allowed any further until you tell me your exact business.'

'He won't talk; says it's private,' said rhino-face, while picking something up from the ground with his long trunk.

'No business is private from me,' said the indoor sentry. 'I am Hermiza's private secretary. Do you understand?'

Potatodai's pulse started to race. He had one chance and could not afford to make any slip-ups.

After taking a very deep breath, Potatodai spoke in a loud assertive voice. 'My name is Kupolas and I am from a planet two hundred miles beneath us called Mecx.'

'And what is the nature of your business?' asked the indoor sentry. *'I would like to rent some land on your planet. We have lots of new babies and ours has become too small,'* lied Potatodai once again. *'We would love to have a holiday home away from our own planet.'*

The sentry pointed to a small hut outside the main door. *'Sit there and wait,'* he instructed *'I will not be long. I will come and let you know if our master wants to see you or not.'*

'Thank you kindly,' mumbled Potatodai, his voice quivering with fright. He considered running away but he realised that this was a very cowardly thing to do. He had come this far so he must continue with what he had to do, regardless of the consequences. He was even willing to give his own life to save his Princess and his planet.

Finally, the sentry came back. *'This way,'* he snorted and they made their way up a staircase covered in the finest golden carpet. It was soft and warm. It reminded Potatodai of the carpet little Jason had on his bedroom floor down on Earth. The heavily armed sentry knocked in a coded fashion on an iron door. Another sentry with a hyena head opened it.

'How many more sentries have I to go through?' thought Potatodai nervously. *'They really do guard their ruler.'* He hoped Aspalemon and the Ziggercraft were safe. If they were gone, his mission and possibly his life were over.

'No, no, no!' he scolded himself. *'I shall not think bad things. If I just think good things, then only good things will happen. I went to Planet Earth and came back in one piece, didn't I?'*

Hermiza, the ruler of Planet Tilahita was sitting at a round table drinking a glass of something that had a very sickening smell.

'Would you like a swig, Mr Kupolas?' he asked. Potatodai immediately thanked him but politely refused.

'It smells horrible and it could be drugged,' he thought to himself.

'Tell me the nature of your business. I hear you want to rent some land. Is this correct?' asked Hermiza. 'Who told you that we might have land for rent, Mr Kupolas? Whoever gave you that information is telling you fibs. We have no land to rent or to sell.'

'No, Mr Hermiza, sir,' answered Potatodai in a low voice. 'We just thought you might have some because your planet is the biggest of all the planets around–'

Potatodai suddenly froze with fear as he felt the back of his babygro suit slowly splitting. One of the seams had burst open, and his potato body was revealed.

'I knew it!' Hermiza roared upon hearing the rip. 'I knew there was something fishy going on. Somebody from a planet so far down the sky would never come up here looking for land. You are one of the Zibazilians. I had a feeling that you looked familiar. Take that stupid thing off you. Ha! But of course, I recognise you now. You are the sentry who sits out by night. You have cut away the daisies from your head.

'I often passed by and felt sorry for you sitting there. Now, you have the nerve to stand here and lie to me. I certainly will not feel sorry for you anymore. Tell me the truth!' he roared. 'Tell me what exactly you are after. You should know that my soldiers are armed and that they will shoot you and all your people at one point of my finger. Do you understand?'

Potatodai's voice trembled as he spoke. 'Please release them, Mr Hermiza sir. Please release Princess Zamba and Carrotpeaash and Turnipear.'

Potatodai knew that he had no choice but to be honest. Even if he ended up in prison, they might release the others. 'Please don't take over our planet,' he begged.

Hermiza hollered with laughter. *'Is that what you lot think?'* he asked. *'Do you really think that a powerful weapon-carrying planet like ours would bother taking over a tiny planet like yours? Zibazila is so small that I could swallow it in one bite,'* he jeered. *'Our sentries could knock it over with their trunks. Why would we bother?*

'I have great respect for your Princess and I would never kidnap her. I did hear what had happened and I had a feeling that one of you would be coming to visit me. Somebody told me about the nasty rumours that Jackus Frostus had been spreading.

'I will forgive you, potato face. You are very brave for risking your life to save your home.'

'Thank you,' whispered Potatodai, ever so meekly.

'When you do find the Princess, give her my best regards, and ask her to come here for a drink some evening. Now if you will excuse me, I have to go and punish somebody who made a mess of polishing our suits of armour. I bid you farewell.'

Hermiza then proceeded to leave the room accompanied by the rhino.

Potatodai felt this may have been a trick to get rid of him, but he was not quite sure. His beloved Princess, Carrotpeaash and Turnipear were probably locked up in a room very close to him. He had to think fast.

'I have brought some earthlings up with me to Zibazilia,' he lied, hoping that this would frighten off the Tilahitan army from coming to Zibazilia. *'They are over six feet tall,'* he boasted.

Neither Hermiza nor his sentries responded. After a long silence, Hermiza lifted his hand in farewell. *'Time will tell the truth,'* he said. *'Time tells everything. I just have a word of warning for you before you go. There are many other planets out there and lots of strange* creatures in the sky. Do not concentrate solely on planet Tilahita just because we have guns. Somebody else may have kidnapped them. Good bye and good luck to you. Your bravery is to be admired. You are a good ambassador for your planet.'

Aspalemon was waiting anxiously for Potatodai's return. He had left the engine of the Ziggercraft running in case he had to take off fast. *'At last!'* he gasped with a great sigh of relief as he saw Potatodai running toward him. *'I thought you had been kidnapped too. Your disguise is ripped. Did the Tilahitans do this to you?'*

'I'm okay, thanks, but I'm in a big muddle,' answered Potatodai. *'Somebody is telling me fibs but I don't know who. We have been to see Jackus Frostus and he does not have the prisoners. He even offered to help us. Now we have looked in Tilahita and they tell me they are not here either. Their leader recognised me and let on to be very angry with me for not trusting his people. All we can do is go back to Zibazilia. Snizzlezallig may have heard something.*

'It's useless, this whole thing. It is like looking for a needle floating in space. I feel like giving up.'

Aspalemon did not answer. Potatodai suddenly froze. *'Surely not! Surely Aspalemon, my trusted pilot, had nothing to do with this kidnapping,'* he thought. No, his imagination was running away with him. Aspalemon probably had nothing to say because he too was so confused with the whole mess. Everything had turned in to such a terrible mess. Potatodai felt his head spinning.

Snizzlezallig was tired, hungry, cold and miserable when the Ziggercraft finally arrived back.

'I got it into my heady that you were never ever coming back,' she moaned. *'I thought that any minute the Tilahitan army would come and take over the place and that I was doomy doomed!'*

She was even more miserable when she heard about their trip.

'He saw through my disguise,' wailed Potatodai. *'He said we should have trusted them and that we blamed them in the wrong. I do not know whether they are playing games with me or not.'*

'Say no more,' hissed Snizzlezallig quietly. *'Jackus Frostus is approaching. I can feel a chill going through my bones.'*

'Sss! Do you have any news?' Jackus called down to the assembled audience. *'Hey, sentry, why are you dressed like that. Isn't it a bad time to be playing games? Anyway, listen I have come to help. I have some more news.'*

'We don't want any help and we certainly don't want anymore of your ideas,' roared Potatodai, trying to keep his eyes focused on Jackus as he moved backwards and forwards in the sky. *'You said that the Tilahitans had taken our Princess and the bodyguards. They just told us that they have not. Somebody is playing games with us and we are sick of it.'*

But now that Jackus Frostus had their attention, he had no intention of shutting up.

'Well, I now have some new information. I saw your Ziggercraft coming back from Tilahita and I guessed you had not succeeded, so I decided to fly there myself.'

Potatodai was a little shocked to find that Jackus had actually made such an effort. 'And what exactly happened when you got there?' he asked.

Jackus flew down a little closer so everybody could hear him clearly. 'Gewq, one of the retired Tilahitan soldiers, told me himself that they are holding your Princess, and the fat and the thin bodyguards, in a dark dungeon under their palace.'

'And, why would he give you this information?' asked Aspalemon. 'I know loads of people in the sky from flying the baby Ziggercraft here and there. I know that everybody dislikes you for your nasty ways. Horrible people do not turn nice without notice. Is there something you are not telling us, Jackus Frostus?'

Jackus suddenly vanished before he had time to answer the question.

'His icicles must have detected some sort of trouble,' Aspalemon explained. 'They were standing straight up. Maybe Glitterati is on his way over here to give him a telling off!'

Snizzlezallig began to cry. 'I want to go home,' she sniffled. 'I want to go home to Gizo. I do not care if they make me wash the magic potion pot for the rest of my life. This is all getting too scaaary. Come with me, spud,' she begged Potatodai. 'Come and live with us witches. We are not the worst, you know, and you will be safe with us. I will makey sure that they never turn you in to a rat or a football again.'

Potatodai urged the now petrified witch to stay calm and did his best to assure her everything would be alright. 'We need you. We need all the help we can get right now,' he said. 'Please, Snizzle, do not leave us now. When Jackus Frostus retreats from battle then it is a big warning sign. Have a look into space, Snizzlezallig; can you see if there is anyone approaching?'

Snizzlezallig perched herself on the top of a high rock to have a look. Her long warty nose got longer and longer, and her beady eyes wore a bulbous look. *'Oh, yes! Yes!'* she cackled excitedly. *'There is something going on.'* Her face had brightened up considerably. *'Looky over there,'* she exclaimed. *'It's our friends the e-mails. There is the Love Mail, and the Birthday Mail, the Holiday Mail, and lots of others. They seem to be circling all around the cave of Jackus Frostus. Come up onto this rock this instant. Look!'*

Potatodai's heart began to thump with excitement. *'Aspalemon, Aspalemon!'* he yelled. *'Please take us out in the Ziggercraft to see what is going on.'*

Aspalemon grabbed his helmet and they all bundled into the Ziggercraft. Everything was in chaos when they got to the cave. They could hear many angry voices.

'Amouras, it's us!' cried Potatodai. *'What is going on?'*

'Oh hi, Potatodai,' he grinned. *'You are about to witness a dramatic rescue.'*

Potatodai gasped with astonishment. *'What kind of rescue? Have you found the Princess and the bodyguards? We are dying to know what is going on.'*

Amouras looked chuffed to be the centre of attention. *'About an hour ago I was passing this way, minding my own business, when I thought I heard a muffled scream. I saw some strands of golden hair blowing out the front of Jackus Frostus's cave.*

I said to myself, "That must be the missing Princess trying to escape." Everybody in the sky knows about the kidnapping. That Glitterati fellow told his stars to spread the word.'

'Tell us more,' begged Aspalemon. 'This is all so exciting.'

Amouras smiled and continued. *'As I came closer, Jackus Frostus shot through the sky and roared at the little Princess and she disappeared into the cave again. Lucky enough, Jackus did not realise I was watching and listening to everything. The Princess has been hidden in a secret compartment in the cave all along. I think Jackus froze her, but she thawed out and tried to escape.'*

'Well hickly, hokly, pokly!' screeched Snizzlezallig excitedly. *'We must get her and the bodyguards out of there.'*

'It's all been taken care of,' answered Amouras. *'I have asked all the e-mails on duty tonight to come here. I asked Liame to allow them off work for a few minutes as a special favour. I do hope he will oblige. I am expecting them in the next five minutes. Maybe Liame will come up himself to see all the action.'*

'And what will you all do?' asked Potatodai. *'Will they be able to rescue Carrotpeaash and Turnipear as well? They are obviously in there with Princess Zamba. They have never done me any favours, but I would not like to see them coming to any harm. They have looked after the Princess so well and that is all that is important to me.'*

Amouras blushed with pride and explain his plan. *'All the e-mails will bounce very hard on the part of the cave that juts out from the sky. The noise will be so loud that Jackus will have to come out, or at least let his prisoners free so that it will stop.'*

'No, no, no!' said Potatodai. *'You must not do that. Jackus Frostus can freeze you all in seconds. If he does, it will take hours to thaw you out and then you will be hours late for work.'*

'But there's something you probably don't know,' laughed the cocky little e-mail.

Potatodai was full of wonder. 'And what is that?' he asked.

'We may be small, but the underside of our bodies, which we use to balance ourselves up in the air, is made of a strong steel material that is frost-resistant.

'That is why we can work right through the winter. Jackus Frostus used to freeze us, and he was our enemy for years. Then we got these steel things attached to our bottoms and we outwitted him.'

Five minutes passed, and Amouras was a little disappointed when he found that only ten e-mails had arrived.

One of them explained: 'We have only twenty-three e-mails working tonight, as earthlings don't send many messages during the night. Thirteen of the twenty-three were too scared to come.'

Amouras was not to be put off. He instructed the ten brave e-mails to jump onto the top part of the cave that jutted out into the sky. Then, jumped up and down, up and down, their steel bottoms making a thunderous sound. A few more e-mails joined the gang, and the clanging continued for over half an hour.

'Something has to crack soon,' whispered Aspalemon. 'Jackus Frostus is not used to this kind of pressure.'

To their surprise, Jackus did not budge. Perhaps he wasn't there. He may have suspected something and left.

'Maybe he has a secret escape passage,' suggested someone, but others disagreed and said there were no secret passages at the top of the sky.

A horn sounded somewhere in the distance.

'*What's that?*' everyone asked, jumping back in shock. The noise came closer, and suddenly an army of about fifty weird-looking creatures dressed in armour came into view.

'*It's the Tilahitans!*' gasped Potatodai, frozen in fear. '*They are on their way to take over Zibazilia! So they were lying to me. Quick, Aspalemon! Start up the Ziggercraft. The e-mails must have been in on this!*'

Every single inhabitant of Planet Zibazilia was alerted as soon as the Ziggercraft sped its way across the sky. The e-mails had pleaded with the crew to wait but they were not willing to listen.

'Grab everything you can to defend yourself,' instructed Potatodai.

'We are going to die,' wailed the smaller Zibazilians. *'What did we do to deserve this? It's not fair.'*

The medical e-mail

For what seemed like ages, they sat in wait, crying their little hearts out. They all knew that they didn't have a hope of winning against the Tilahitan army but each one was willing to try their very best.

Eventually, a horn tooted in the distance. The Tilahitans had finally arrived to take over their beloved planet. Potatodai braced himself and went outside.

'Take me as a prisoner but do not take my planet,' he begged on his knees. *'I will be your servant forever and ever.'* His head was bowed and tears streamed from his eyes. *'Take me, I beg you.'*

But Potatodai was in for the surprise of his life.

'Raise yourself, potato,' ordered a senior Tilahitan warrior. *'You have got it all wrong. We have come to rescue the Princess and her bodyguards. Our instructions are from our ruler, Hermiza. He was so impressed with your courage that he has decided to help. He likes the people of Zibazilia and they have never once caused him any trouble.'*

Potatodai was astonished. *'I'm sorry,'* he cried, blubbing like a baby. *'Please convey that message to your ruler. Tell him I am sorry for doubting him. How could we have been taken in by Jackus Frostus like that?'*

'We were all taken in,' said a voice from behind. Glitterati had arrived accompanied by Luna the moon. *'We too believed all his lies. We thought he had changed. We all fell for it. '*

The e-mails, meanwhile, had flown over to Zibazilia and were hovering in the sky, waiting for further instructions. A few more had joined the group.

'And to think you didn't trust us, Potatodai!' one of them cried. *'Always get your facts right before you lay blame. Now, let us all go*

over there together. A couple of dozen trunks and some steel bottoms should make a loud enough racket. He will have to come out sooner or later.'

Potatodai blew a space kiss towards the e-mails. *'I'm sorry I doubted you,'* he sobbed. *'I should have known that you were all my good friends. Only for you lot, I would never have been to Planet Earth. Let's go, everybody. We have a job to do.'*

Jackus Frostus did not intend to give in. From a peephole in the wall of his cave, he spied the army approaching Planet Zibazilia and knew it was only a matter of time before they came over to his cave. His nerves were already rattled after listening to the e-mails pounding on his cave. Now the Tilahitans were coming. He had to think fast – faster than ever before.

He furiously oiled his spikes, ready for action. *'Watch out, everybody,'* yelled Potatodai from behind the Ziggercraft. *'Watch out, warriors, Frostus is coming to freeze you!'*

One spike came out of the cave, and then two, and then three. Suddenly everything got very cold. Potatodai, Snizzlezallig and Aspalemon ran for cover, but the Tilahitan army could not run fast enough and their trunks froze to their heads. That meant they could not fire their ammunition.

'Tee, hee, hee,' sniggered Jackus Frostus nastily. *'It will take hours for them to defrost. They will have to wait till the sun comes out; there is no other way of melting the ice.'*

However, while Jackus Frostus was busy pointing his rays at everybody, trying to freeze them, somebody else was thinking hard. One smart Tilahitan sentry had a secret weapon inside his trunk. It was a space heater used by the night sentries to keep warm in winter. The sentry knew that Jackus would try to freeze them. He shook and shook his trunk until the heater fell out.

Inside the cave, Princess Zamba had heard all the commotion and was waiting for her chance to escape. She was shaking from head to toe, hoping that nobody would get hurt. She crept from her secret compartment at the bottom of the cave and shook the stiffness out of her legs. Finally she stuck her head out the door of the cave.

'No, no, Your Highness!' yelled Potatodai. 'Stay in the cave for now. If you come out, Frostus will freeze you too.'

A quick-thinking e-mail heard his plea and responded with lightning speed. This was the Health Mail, who was very fit and could move super fast.

'Catch on to the side of me, Princess,' he called out as he bent down over the roof of the cave.

'I'm too small,' cried the Princess. 'I can't reach you.'

Before anybody had time to think, the Health Mail grabbed a big bunch of the Princess's golden hair and lifted her quickly aboard. They were high up in the sky before Jackus Frostus had time to realise what was happening.

'What about Carrotpeaash and Turnipear?' asked Aspalemon. 'Should we try to rescue them now?'

'Later, later,' replied Potatodai. 'I will make sure they are rescued. First, we will get the Princess back to Zibazilia. We will come back to rescue them. The Tilahitans will guard the cave until then. I am not heartless enough to leave them. I hope one day that they will repay me.'

However, Jackus Frostus was not finished. Even though he was in a terrible daze and his head was spinning, he leapt on to the back of the Ziggercraft in which Potatodai, Aspalemon and the Princess were travelling.

Aspalemon nearly lost control of the craft with the fright. *'We are all doomed,'* he gasped. *'He will freeze us to death.'*

'No he won't,' said Potatodai firmly. He was now fairly calm and able to think properly. *'He can't freeze our craft because he can't freeze anything with steel in it. The only problem we will have is getting out of the craft and into our palace. He can freeze us then.'*

Suddenly Potatodai let out a roar. *'Where is Snizzlezallig?'*

'*Thanks for the lift, guys,*' roared Jackus through the Ziggercraft window as they approached Planet Zibazilia. '*Now either you come out and I will freeze you or you will rot inside your craft. Tee, hee, hee! I bet you did not think to bring some food and space juice with you, did you? Haha!*'

Princess Zamba cried and cried and cried. She was crying so much that nobody understood a word of what she was trying to say. Strawberry-shaped tears poured from her beautiful eyes.

'*Potatodai, I have just had the most brilliant brainwave!*' squealed Aspalemon out of the blue. '*Signal the e-mails to come over here and tell them to surround the Ziggercraft. Frostus will not be able to freeze us if we are surrounded by their steel bottoms.*'

Potatodai thumped him on the back good-humouredly. '*And there I was thinking I was the only one on Zibazilia who had brains,*' he joked.

The Ziggercraft landed, followed closely by the e- mails, who were chanting together in the sky. '*We saved the day, we saved the day,*' they sang. '*We rescued the Princess! Now we will save the bodyguards.*'

'*It's not over yet,*' growled Jackus Frostus. '*Just you lot wait and see.*'

Everybody was surprised to find him in such a good humour. '*What is he up to?*' they wondered.

'*Put out the drawbridge now,*' Jackus yelled. '*Put out the bridge.*'

'Who is he shouting at?' everybody asked. *'Has he gone crazy?'*

Suddenly a tiny window opened in the north wing of the Zibazilians' palace, and to everyone's amazement, out peered Carrotpeaash and Turnipear, who beamed from ear to ear.

'What the heck is going on?' stammered Potatodai. *'How did they get there?'*

Princess Zamba burst into another flood of tears.

'I couldn't come back the day I said I would because there were so many snoops around,' Jackus roared over to the two bodyguards. *'So now can you please put the bridge out and let me into the palace.'*

Everybody froze in silence as the terrible truth began to dawn on them. Jackus Frostus was working with Carrotpeaash and Turnipear all along. They had planned to take over Planet Zibazilia and to leave Princess Zamba to die in the cave.

'Let me in, boys,' Jackus called again to Carrotpeaash and Turnipear, but to everyone's surprise they did not budge.

Finally, Carrotpeaash lifted up a space microphone and said to Jackus. *'Do you take us for fools, Jackus Frostus? You told us that if we helped you to get the Princess out of here that the three of us would rule Planet Zibazilia. We want you to know that we never believed you. You do not know how to tell the truth.'*

'I did mean it, I did mean it!' roared Jackus. *'You both helped to mastermind the kidnapping of the Princess by sending Potatodai to Planet Earth. Only for you, I could not have got her to my cave. I intend to make you both joint rulers of Planet Zibazilia with me. The three of us will rule the planet.'*

'If you do, then why is the Princess sitting in the Ziggercraft now?'

bellowed Turnipear. *'The whole idea was that she would die in your cave and nobody would ever find her.'*

'I can sort it out,' Jackus quivered. *'We will banish her to the cellars and make her a slave. Or … or … if you so wish I will organise for her to have a terrible accident. We could even throw her into space and let her fall forever and ever. Tee, hee, hee. That is such a lovely thought. A Strawberry Princess falling for the rest of time.'*

'You are all talk and no action, Jackus Frostus. Well, we have news for you. We never wanted you to rule Planet Zibazilia. We hate your guts. We used you. We knew that if we kidnapped the Princess ourselves that our elders would put a curse on us. We also knew that Potatodai and that stupid witch were watching us and we did not want them to suspect anything.

'Anyway, you blew it, Jackus Frostus,' yelled Carrotpeaash. *'We are now the new rulers of Planet Zibazilia. Everybody in that Ziggercraft is now banished from this planet.'*

PrIncess Zamba wailed. *'You were my trusted bodyguards,'* she cried. *'Poor Potatodai was banished to sentry duty for all those years just because I listened to you two. I always knew that should not have happened.'*

Carrotpeaash and Turnipear almost bent in two as they laughed and laughed out of the window. *'We did it!'* they howled. *'We are now the proud rulers of Planet Zibazilia. Everybody must now answer to us. No more of that stupid Strawberry Princess annoying us if her hair gets wet or if her golden slippers are scuffed. It was worth putting up with her for so long,'* they tittered together.

'And as for that spuddy-face sentry, we can use him for a slave,' Carrotpeaash roared with laughter. *'And that stupid ugly witch, we will cut her up in to bits and have some Snizzle soup. I hope it smells better than she does now.'*

Turnipear joined in: 'I can't wait to taste it,' he scoffed. 'It will be such a treat. Have a nice life, everybody; we, the new rulers of Zibazilia, are off to fill our tummies with the best food from the larder.'

While all of this was going on, another e-mail was circling unnoticed in the background. With him, he carried two very important passengers.

When Snizzlezallig had first discovered what was happening she acted fast. She sent a message with an elf over to the e-mail canteen and, lo and behold, there was Furryfuzz, the Animal Rescue Mail, having a bite to eat.

'This is all either a stroke of luck or else it was all meant to be,' she thought joyfully. Furryfuzz finished his drink and discreetly flew over to where the frightened witch was hiding.

Snizzlezallig hurriedly told him her story and begged him to assist. He nodded and she quickly jumped on his back. They headed in the direction of Planet Earth at enormous speed. She held her broomstick tightly in her hand as they approached the e-mail tunnel.

She hoped Gizo was not prowling the sky. She just did not have time to explain everything to her. She hadn't even had time to tell Potatodai she was leaving. He would be so worried. Anyway, it was too late now for second thoughts. She had a plan and she had to make sure it worked.

Jason was asleep in bed when she arrived, but his big black tom cat Oxo was not. Oxo was roaming the alleys looking for a girlfriend. Before Oxo had time to blink, Snizzlezallig had grabbed his long furry tail and put him on the back of her broomstick. He tried spitting and hissing but he was far too shocked to claw his kidnapper as they quickly sped towards the e-mail tunnel.

As agreed, Furryfuzz, the Animal Rescue Mail, was waiting at the tunnel and the three of them shot through the sky at tremendous speed toward the doomed planet of Zibazilia. Even Old Man Time gasped as they passed by. It was the strangest thing he had ever recorded in all his millions of years of recording. He had just witnessed an e-mail carrying a witch and a big furry black earthling cat. He wondered what was going on. Maybe he should call an emergency meeting of his space council. The stars would let him know what was happening later.

So much had changed since Snizzlezallig had left. The Ziggercraft was on the ground outside the palace. Jackus Frostus was lying behind a rock, cursing and spitting. Two Tilahitans with super-long trunks were threatening to shoot him if he dared lift one of his icy spikes.

'Our entire army is on the way over here,' they warned him. Jackus Frostus appeared to have lost his will to fight. Everything had gone so wrong. Now everybody would hate him even more than they already had.

The e-mails clung to the steel bottom of the Ziggercraft. The crew and the sobbing Princess remained inside.

Carrotpeaash and Turnipear were laughing out the window. *'We have won,'* they sang. *'Revenge is such a sweet thing. We are now kings of this castle, dum, de, dum!'*

Princess Zamba sobbed loudly and banged her strawberry fists with rage against the windows of the Ziggercraft.

'Go where you like you silly Strawberry Princess,' gloated Carrotpeaash. *'I am tired of looking after your daft needs. Who ever heard of anyone having to clean a mirror tied on to someone's shoe so as they could look at themselves?'*

'And I won't have to sleep outside your silly bedroom door on guard all night,' mocked Turnipear.

'We are the rulers of Zibazilia,' they sang. *'We are the rulers of Zibazilia. Dum de dum, diddly ya ya yo!'*

Snizzlezallig sat in the background for a few moments as she did her best to piece together everything that had happened while she was down on Planet Earth. Oxo the cat lay cuddled up under her heavy black cloak. His nails were sharp, and she longed to put him on the ground.

'Coooeee, it's meee,' cackled Snizzlezallig as she finally crept her way in through the back door of the Ziggercraft. I've brought some helpy.'

Potatodai gasped as he felt something large and very hairy rubbing against him. It was making a loud purring noise.

'That earthling cat belongs to Jason!' he gasped. *'How did you manage to get him?'*

'Haha!' giggled Snizzlezallig. *'I'm smarter than you thinky. I may be ugly, but I have brains to burn. I thinky quickly when I have to.'*

'Okay, okay!' chuckled Potatodai. *'I believe you. Right, Snizzle let the action begin.'*

'I will need your help,' cooed Snizzlezallig happily. *'I'm not sure if this Oxo cat is up to saving a planet on his own.'*

'It's our last chance,' said Potatodai. *'Let's go for it.'*

'Now, Oxo!' Snizzlezallig yelled to the big black cat, who was swishing his tail like a mad thing. *'Go, cat, go!'*

And with that signal, Oxo made one giant leap onto the rock where Jackus Frostus lay. There was a loud hiss.

'He has punctured Jackus Frostus so he won't be able to freeze us again!' cheered the crowd.

'That's what you get for puncturing my nose,' shouted Snizzlezallig. *'What goes aroundy comes around.'*

'This will take months to mend,' groaned Jackus Frostus. *'Half the winter will be over before I can go back to work again. Do not be too hard on me. Turnipear and Carrotpeaash plotted the whole thing. They have been dying to take over Planet Zibazilia for ages. That is why they banished Potatodai; they were worried that someday the Princess would make him ruler because he is so smart.'*

'Shut it, Frostus,' someone replied. *'We have heard enough from you for one day, in fact we have heard enough from you for a whole lifetime.'*

Jackus Frostus was now out of the picture. He puffed and panted his way back to his cave. His punctured body pained badly, and he looked a terrible sight.

But the gates of Planet Zibazilia remained closed, and Potatodai, Aspalemon, and the Princess were getting desperate. Carrotpeaash and Turnipear refused to budge.

'Jackus Frostus has gone,' yelled Aspalemon. *'Please come out and talk to us. We will all come to some agreement. The Princess has a very forgiving nature.'*

'You can keep the Ziggercraft,' shouted one of the bodyguards. *'Go anywhere you like but you are not getting back here. We have had all the locks changed and the Zibazilians are now under our control.'*

The atmosphere was very tense. The Tilahitan army paced over and back. They decided against using their weapons in case they might destroy the beautiful Zibazilian Palace. In addition to that, some of the Zibazilians could have been caught in the crossfire.

Several of the e-mails had left, as they had urgent messages to deliver. Glitterati was keeping a low profile but was busy thinking behind the scenes. He was not going to let his favourite planet go without a big, big fight.

He sent word that the hundreds of stars who had the night off must come back into the sky, and as each arrived, he gave them their instructions. He gave each cluster of stars a letter just as he had done on the night of the kidnapping.

Glitterati hoped and prayed that little Jason would be watching from Earth. Luckily, he was. Oxo usually came back from roaming in the middle of the night; he would squeeze through the quarter-opened window and plonk himself down on the bottom of the bed.

Jason had woken and noticed his beloved cat was not there. Only for that, he would never have noticed the very, very important message waiting for him zillions of miles up in the sky.

His curtains were open, so he stretched his head as far as he could to see the huge number of stars lighting up the sky. His tummy churned with excitement.

'It's a message,' he gasped. 'A secret message just for me.

'Send as many different e-mail messages as you can,' it read. 'We need more e-mails up here urgently. They cannot come up unless they have a message to carry. We are in trouble. Help!'

Jason had one very big problem. It was still the middle of the night and he was unable to get out of bed to use his computer. He would have to wake his parents for help. What would he tell them? The Zibazilians needed his help urgently so a wrong move could be fatal.

'Dad,' he called out. 'Dad, could you come in for a minute please?'

His sleepy dad finally arrived at his door looking worried. 'What is it, son? What's happened?'

'It's an essay I have to do for school!' Jason lied. 'I forgot all about it and another chap and I have to read ours out in the morning. I need to sit at the computer and do it now.'

His father grinned, wondering if he was hearing things. 'Jason, this is the first time you have ever shown such interest in your homework, and especially in the middle of the night. Are you sure you're not just coming out of a bad dream?'

But Jason was adamant, so his father wrapped a rug around him and positioned his wheelchair beside the computer.

He breathed a sigh of relief as his bemused father left the room. What would happen if his father asked to read the essay in the morning? Oh, what the heck, he would worry about that in the morning. He had other things to do right now. Planet Zibazilia needed him.

He didn't know why the stars wanted him to do this, but he did it anyway. He sent e-mail after e-mail to everybody he could think of, saying happy birthday, congratulations, new baby, happy Christmas, ordering takeaways, and lots more. He would have a lot of explaining to do tomorrow but he didn't care.

The plan worked. E-mail after e-mail left Jason's computer and flew through the sky. As each of them turned at the top of the sky, they were stopped by Locko the Security Mail and told not to move any further.

'What are you lot shivering about?' yelled Locko. *'You are all cowards! You need to toughen up. The little Princess is in trouble and we are going to help her.'*

'But – but the earthlings will not be happy,' cried one e-mail.

'The earthlings will only be too happy to help a planet in need,' answered Locko.

A large number of e-mails had now congregated in the sky, as word passed from one to the other of what was going on. They all moaned and complained.

'We will be sacked,' someone groaned.

'What about our important messages?' whined another, but the Security Mail assured them that everything would be fine.

'Trust me,' he stated, with a big air of importance. *'Liame and I are good buddies. The boss knows I can be trusted. I will take the blame if any of you get into trouble.'*

Hearing this, the e-mails began to relax and chatted amongst themselves, awaiting further orders.

The Security Mail chatted with Glitterati and everyone assembled for a long few minutes. Everybody offered their own suggestions as to what they should do. They were all Impressed when Snizzlezallig came up with a smart but rather daring plan.

'*Drop me and Oxo the cat down at the side door of the palace,*' Snizzlezallig instructed Furryfuzz, the Animal Rescue Mail. '*Tell the other e-mails to keep Carrotpeaash and Turnipear occupied so they won't notice me.*'

Snizzlezallig quickly emptied the laundry bag that Potatodai had brought from Planet Earth and tied her smelly black cloak around it. Oxo the cat sat on her shoulders, purring loudly and licking his lips.

'*Let the Princess rule! Let her rule!*' chanted the crowd. '*She's the greatest, she's the best.*'

By this time, more and more e-mails had arrived on the scene. Jason had been very busy.

'*You lot, get out of the sky,*' roared Turnipear out of a window high up in the palace.

'*He's in the Princess's chambers,*' sobbed Potatodai. '*That means that they have taken over. Keep on shouting, everybody, and he will be distracted. Tilahitans, please bang your trunks on the ground. Make loads of noise.*'

Carrotpeaash then growled out the window: '*We are rulers now and you e-mails are forbidden to come near here. Take the contents of your silly little canteen and get out of here. Take the Princess, the witch and that silly billy sentry Potatodai with you. As for you Tilahitans, if you use your weapons you will blow up the palace, and then our powers will kick in and you will all die. Haha!*'

As Carrotpeaash roared, the e-mails rubbed their little tummies and laughed. The more they laughed, the madder Carrotpeaash got.

'You lot can laugh, and you lot in the Ziggercraft can too, but none of you are getting in here,' he jeered. *'Turnipear and I rule this planet now. We are changing its name from Zibazilia to Planet Carroturn.'*

'Yes, that's right. We are calling it after ourselves,' mocked Turnipear.

The e-mails laughed louder and louder and louder. Everybody in the Ziggercraft laughed, Glitterati and his stars laughed, and the Tilahitan army banged their trunks and made a huge racket. The sky rocked with the sound of laughter and noise.

As the distraction continued outside, Snizzlezallig hurriedly pushed Oxo the cat under the big back door of the palace. She knew that his weight and strength would weaken the door.

At the same time, Snizzlezallig began to grate down the hinges with the cheese grater that Potatodai had brought from Planet Earth. It was hard work, but she was getting there. She wiped the sweat from her face with her cape.

Finally, she was in. She knew it was only a matter of minutes before Carrotpeaash and Turnipear would notice her. Oxo licked his lips, wagged his tail, and waited for further instructions. This was better than any late-night romp around his neighbourhood.

Snizzlezallig put the cat on her shoulders, and slowly they crept upstairs. Oxo began hissing loudly.

'It's not a mousey we are after, Oxo, but have fun anyway,' whispered Snizzlezallig. *'These two bodyguards are far worse than any mice. They are a pair of sneaky rats. Off you go now. Have a great time!'*

The top floor was deserted. Carrotpeaash and Turnipear had obviously instructed everybody to stay down underground in case of trouble. They were also worried that some of the pages might revolt and try to rescue the Princess.

Slowly, Snizzlezallig crept down the landing. This was her moment. Very, very quietly, she set four large mouse traps Potatodai had taken from Jason's school.

'Thank you once again for this bag of stuffy wuffy, earthling Jason,' she whispered to herself. *'And thank you, Potatodai for having the brains to bring them from Planet Earth. You trusted me to mind them for you, so I hope I am going to do you proud. Maybe after all this you will give me a kissy.'*

Slowly, and with the greatest of care, Snizzlezallig covered the ground in front of her with sticky gnat juice and glue.

She then poured the box of Earth Rice Krispies over the sticky mixture. Finally she poured out Jason's milk. As she did so, the Rice krispies began to snap, crackle and pop and make an awful loud noise.

'Not long now,' grinned Snizzlezallig, as she and Oxo hid behind a bench.

She was right. Carrotpeaash and Turnipear rushed in, shouting. *'Is that gunfire? Oh no, the Tilahitans must be shooting at the palace! Let's go down to the dungeon and hide.'*

As they came closer, the snap, crackle and pops of the Rice Krispies became louder and louder.

'We are being shot at!' they screeched *'Where are the bullets coming from? How did anyone get in here?'*

Things were about to get a lot worse for the bodyguards. They both screamed in pain as the set mousetraps sprang into action. They were trapped. Snizzlezallig rushed forward and tied them together with a roll of fishing line from Jason's laundry bag. Little Jason from Planet Earth had certainly been thinking ahead.

Carrotpeaash and Turnipear pulled, dragged, huffed, and puffed, but they could not release themselves from the traps. Oxo stood guard, with his claws sticking out.

'Miaooow!' he cried with delight from time to time. *'Only a matter of time now and I will have my dinner,'* he thought. *'These space creatures look ever so good, especially the fat one.'*

Carrotpeaash and Turnipear both trembled with fear, and after struggling for a while they decided to give up. *'What is that?'* They pointed at Oxo. *'Is it a hairy baby dinosaur?'*

Oxo, insulted after being called a dinosaur, stuck out his claws again and hissed at them.

'Dinosaur my whisker,' he thought. *'You'll regret comparing me to that. You will be very sorry when you are in my tummy. Nobody compares a fine big tom cat to a dinosaur.'*

Snizzlezallig, in the meantime, had been busy. She had gone and found a senior page who had released the bridge across the moat for her. At first, the page was too frightened but on hearing that his beloved Princess was stranded outside he decided to co-operate with the ugly creature.

'Bring the Ziggercraft in,' Snizzlezallig sang out happily. *'Your planet has been saved!'*

Minutes later the main gates swung open and the Ziggercraft slowly entered.

'*Get out of your hiding places, everybody,*' Potatodai shouted. '*This is Potatodai and we have found the Princess. Even though a little frightened, she is alive and well. Carrotpeaash, Turnipear and Jackus Frostus will never make you frightened again. Come out now and welcome the Princess back!*'

There were cheers and tears of joy. Zibazilians ran everywhere, jumping up and down with delight. They kissed, hugged, turned somersaults, and did all the craziest things they could think of. They even raided the main larder for goodies. This larder was normally out of bounds to pages and juniors, but nobody cared on this joyous occasion.

'*Princess Zamba rules again, she rules again,*' sang everybody outside.

'*Hear, hear,*' sang the Zibazilians in utter delight after they had heard the full story.

'*Let's have a party,*' yelled Princess Zamba, who felt very tired but was also in really high spirits. '*Bring everybody in here, including all the e-mails, and the Tilahitan army, and of course Glitterati and the stars. Snizzlezallig, please ask one of the pages to prepare the finest dish for that earthling cat. This planet and this palace could do with some visitors. I always took advice from Carrotpeaash and Turnipear and now I do not have to anymore.*'

'*Hear, hear,*' cheered all assembled.

'*Shh! I have not finished what I had to say,*' giggled Princess Zamba. '*From now on, all our neighbouring planets and the e-mails are our friends. I intend to change the name Planet Zibazilia to Planet Fun. Let us eat, drink, dance, and have that fun. Yibbly yi yall, yum yum yum.*'

Potatodai raised his hand. '*Your Royal Highness, I have one question, if I may ask it please?*'

Princess Zamba walked toward him. *'I am all ears, dear Potatodai,'* she beamed.

'Your Highness, I think we must find a way to reward the little earthling called Jason who has been so kind and so helpful to us. Without him and his cat, we would have been doomed forever.' Princess Zamba thought and thought, and then thought some more.

Glitterati put up one of his points. *'I think I may have the answer to that, Your Royal Highness.'*

'Please continue,' begged the little Princess.*'I am all ears.'*

'I shall have a word with ten of my brightest stars,' said Glitterati. *'I shall ask them to shine down on Jason's bedroom every single night. I shall also ask Luna the moon to do some breakdancing between the clouds to entertain him.'*

Princess Zamba grinned with delight. *'What wonderful ideas, Glitterati. I shall also have a meeting with all the senior space mechanics and together we will design a super-large Ziggercraft, which will enable us to go up and down to Planet Earth. It will be designed specially to carry the wheelchair thing, and it will allow the little earthling to visit us if he wishes. We will build a special super size bedroom for him '*

'*Marry me, Potatodai,*' whispered Snizzlezallig, rubbing her warty nose against his ear. '*I do not think I have ever met anyone so nice in my whole life. I did it all for you. I helped to save the Princess and your planet. Do you get what I am saying?*'

'*Oh no, she's at it again,*' thought Potatodai. '*Has she not had enough excitement for one day?*'

'*Get away from me. Getting married to a witch is not a cool thing to do,*' mumbled Potatodai. He thought again. '*I'm sorry, Snizzlezallig. I do adore you as my friend and I thank you for your help and bravery. However, I do believe somebody else fancies you, just you wait and see. But there is something very important I have to do. I must be mad, but I am going to do it anyway.*'

The assembled audience became very still.

Potatodai wiped a drop of sweat from his forehead and spoke. '*I must do what I have not had the courage to do before now. It is something I have dreamed of for many, many years. On cold, frosty nights it is the thought has kept me going.*'

'*What is it?*' enquired one of the smallest pages. '*I can't take anymore more excitement! My tiny heart is beating too fast.*'

'*Shh!*' hissed somebody else.

'*Princess Zamba. Dear, sweet Strawberry Princess Zamba of Zibazilia, will you marry me?*' Potatodai asked to the astonishment of everyone.

'Ohhh!' they all gasped in sheer amazement. It was unheard of to make a marriage proposal to a Princess. But now that the bodyguards were tied up and would be banished, Potatodai knew that the Princess was free to make up her own mind about things. *'Potatodai, you can't marry her – you have to marry meee!'* bawled Snizzlezallig.

'Snizzlezallig, as I said already, I love you dearly as a friend and I can't thank you enough for all the help you have given us,' said Potatodai in a very low voice. *'Unfortunately, my heart belongs to someone else, and that is our gorgeous Princess Zamba.'*

'I will marry the witch,' boomed a loud voice from the back of the crowd. Everybody turned around to see Aspalemon the pilot making his way towards her. *'You are so different. I have been hoping for ages that you would noticed me,'* he confessed. *'I could boast to all my friends that my wife is a really clever witch who helped save our planet.'*

Snizzlezallig was dumbfounded. Things were happening so fast she just could not keep track of them herself. *'Well, if the truth be known, I have been watching you from time to time, but I thought you had no interest in meee,'* she confessed.

Aspalemon blushed.

'In facty, Aspa, I have always dreamt of being swept off my feet by a pilot.'

Potatodai chimed in from behind: *'I always suspected that it was Aspalemon that you really loved. I saw the way the two of you looked at each other the first day we met.'*

'Okey doky, holy smokey!' squealed Snizzlezallig with great excitement. *'I will marry you, Mr Pilot. You can be king of the sky down as far as the e-mail tunnel, and I will be queen of the sky from there to Planet Earthy.'*

MADDIE CONWAY

'Marry Potatodai, Princess Zamba,' cheered the e- mails outside in the night sky. *'Marry our friend Potatodai.'*

'Well, I have news for you lot,' grinned the Princess. *'That is exactly what I plan to do. I would love to marry my dear, dear friend who risked his life for me and for the planet.'*

Everybody went crazy. Garter, the Wedding Mail, was the first to congratulate them. The rest of the gang outside went bananas in the sky. Even Liame paid a visit and had a private audience with Princess Zamba. Everybody danced the space hokey-cokey and even did some breakdancing.

A little page handed a piece of paper out the window of the palace. It was read aloud by Aspalemon for all the e-mails present. 'The Princess of Zibazilia – or should we say the Princess of Planet Fun – has been informed of the magnificent help you have given us for the past few months and she now intends to reward you. She has already, as you know, loaned you a canteen on the edge of the planet, but now she is allowing you a piece of our ground which you can claim as your own. When you reach here on your wearying journey, you will now be able to stop for a chat and have something to eat. All the food will be provided free of charge by our chef Peachywillow.

'Thank you, thank you!' said Liame on behalf of all his e-mails. *'For years, we have wanted something like this but we were much too scared to ask. Now all the mails will get a little rest and a private place of their own on their journey. It will make all our lives much easier.'*

'One other thing,' shouted Princess Zamba through the commotion.

'Speak, Princess,' everybody shouted back.

251

'I will arrange for a large plaque to be erected in honour of the wonderful Tilahitan army who have helped us so much. It will be placed at the edge of our planet for everybody to see.'

'What an honour,' whispered Zaza the page to his friend Zope. *'Nobody ever gets a plaque of honour here.'*

'And another surprise for the Tilahitans,' giggled the Princess.

'What's that, Princess?' asked the rhino Tilahitan, while wriggling his long trunk in an excited fashion.

'You now have two brand new slaves, my two former bodyguards, Turnipear and Carrotpeaash. Make sure you work them ever so hard.'

'What a wonderful end for them,' someone whooped from the crowd. *'What about Glitterati and his wonderful stars?'*

'Oh, yes,' answered Princess Zamba. *'I had not forgotten. I have always felt so sorry for all those stars and the tiny cave they live in. Tomorrow there will be a big change. I will give instruction to remove Jackus Frostus from his large sky cave and I will banish him to the smallest cave in the sky. He will no longer be in a position to stretch out his icicles at night, as there will not be room. Glitterati and his stars will be given his cave, and will have loads and loads of extra space.'*

'Well deserved!' answered all assembled.

Princess Zamba's rescue was timed to perfection, as the following Monday the space sky festival commenced. The festival consisted of two nights in the year when all space dwellers came together for fun. A massive tent was tied to the top of the sky and was able to hold almost everybody.

Nobody said any nasty things to each other and everybody forgot their troubles for one night. Even Jackus Frostus and Thundrati the thunder maker made an appearance, though they stayed at opposite ends of the sky. Nobody did any work that night, so the sky was dark for the whole night.

All the junior stars played Ring around the Rosie while the oldies did some space-waltzing. Music was transmitted from a spacecraft that rocked backwards and forwards in the sky.

Princess Zamba looked more radiant than ever and was the centre of attention all night. Despite many requests, she refused to dance and she sat on a golden seat at the edge of her own planet, surrounded by Potatodai and the pages.

Then, huge platters of exciting food arrived. Snizzlezallig and Potatodai offered everybody a small sip of Coca- Cola, which they brought from Planet Earth. Everybody ooohed and aaahed as they felt the fizz, and some became rather light-headed and silly.

Princess Zamba dipped a silver spoon into a piece of zakuaka pie, which was covered in gehr, a peppermint-tasting food something like cream. *'Yum yum,'* she said. *'It's the best one I have ever tasted. I do not intend to leave one single bit.'*

But Potatodai was far too excited to eat. The little Princess had just whispered in his ear that once they had married she would give him the title, *'King of Planet Fun'.*

The space party went on and on and on until everybody collapsed with exhaustion.

Down on Planet Earth, little Jason sat by his window, looking for glimmers of light coming from the tip-top of the sky. Potatodai had told him about the space party so he knew it was in full swing.

Deep down, little Jason was also sure of one other thing. He knew that he had not seen the last of Potatodai. A whole raft of new adventures was about to begin and he could not wait.

Old Man Time stood in the middle of the sky as he listened to the screams of excitement overhead. Recording the happenings in the sky over the past few weeks was going to be a really hard job but there was one thing he knew for sure. He was going to enjoy every single moment of it!

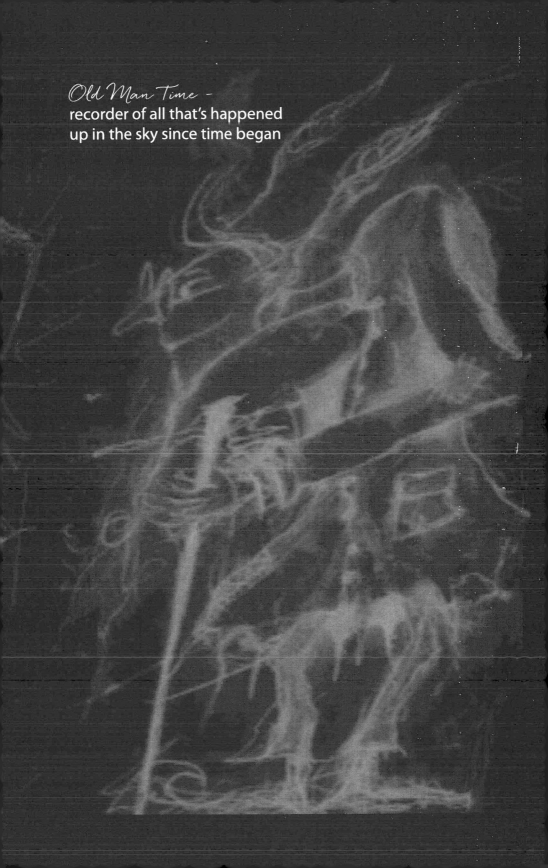

Old Man Time –
recorder of all that's happened
up in the sky since time began

Next Time:

Zibizalians visit Planet Earth!